NOTES
FROM
A LIAR
AND HER
DOG

NOTES FROM A LIAR AND HER DOG

Gennifer Choldenko

BLOOMSBURY

First published in Great Britain in 2002
by Bloomsbury Publishing Plc,
36 Soho Square, London, W1D 3QY

This paperback edition published in 2008

Published in America by Harcourt Books

A CIP catalogue record of this book is available from the British Library

ISBN 978 0 7475 8780 4

Printed and bound in Great Britain by Clays Ltd, St Ives Plc

10 9 8 7 6 5 4 3 2 1

All papers used by Bloomsbury Publishing are natural, recyclable products made
from wood grown in well-managed forests. The manufacturing processes con-
form to the environmental regulations of the country of origin.

www.bloomsbury.com/gennifercholdenko

To
Jacob Ayer Cholden Brown

CONTENTS

1
WOLF

"I don't even know what I did this time," I say to my best friend, Harrison Emerson. We watch my mother park her car in the school's visitor parking slot.

"Could be she's here because of Kate. Maybe Kate's in trouble," Harrison suggests. He is sitting on the asphalt in the shade of the backboard, drawing a chicken in his math book. He always draws during recess, until a noon aide makes him play.

"Oh, right. My little sister's idea of getting in trouble is putting a book back upside down," I say, mopping the sweat off my forehead with the tail of my shirt. I sock the handball hard against the backboard.

"Antonia MacPherson, please come to the office." The loudspeaker sounds patchy and too loud. A kid I don't know screams, "You cheat!" Another kid smacks the tetherball behind me.

"Antonia MacPherson, please come to the office." The loudspeaker lady is mad now, like if she has to walk all the way out to the playground to find me, my butt will be butter.

"Want me to come?" Harrison asks. Harrison is

working on the chicken's wing feathers. I know he hates stopping in the middle of the feather part, but I can't help it. I need him.

"Yeah," I say.

It's been a while since I've been called to the office. I got bored of it, really. The assistant principal, Mr. Borgdorf, always makes everything sound as if it is life or death, like if you put one foot outside the crosswalk, you are headed for the penitentiary. He loves rules. He has them written all fancy and hung on the walls of his office.

We take the long way to Mr. Borgdorf's office, stopping for a drink at the water fountain. The water is hot and tastes like pennies. I get a big mouthful and spit it out on Harrison's shoes. Then Harrison gets a big mouthful and spits it out on my shoes. We are wet up to our knees when Cave Man comes along. Cave Man is our teacher. His real name is Mr. Lewis, but everyone calls him Cave Man because he's all hairy like one of those monkeys in our history book—the ones that walk stooped, then turn into men. Cave Man escorts us to the office.

"Antonia? Is that you?" the assistant principal calls out as soon as he hears us in the main office. He knows me by name. This is not an honor, my mother always says.

"You go first," I tell Harrison.

Harrison nods. Harrison is short. His T-shirt is almost as long as a dress and his cargo pants are dirty and frayed at the bottom from stepping on them.

"Harrison Emerson, why am I not surprised to see

you," my mom says. My mom is sitting in Mr. Borgdorf's office with her legs neatly crossed. She is wearing a work skirt and blouse with a scarf around her neck, held in place with a pin. She is glaring at Harrison. My mom hates Harrison because he eats with his mouth open, walks his pet chicken on a leash, and because he's always scratching at something. I'm not friends with Harrison because my mom doesn't like him, though. I'm friends with him because I like him. That my mom doesn't like him is something extra, like a bonus.

"Hey, Harrison, Ant, how are you two doing today?" asks Just Carol. Just Carol is our art teacher. We call her Just Carol because she always says, "Just call me Carol." Not Miss or Ms. or Mrs. Anything. I wonder what she is doing here.

Harrison blushes so red, his freckles disappear. He loves Just Carol. He has her picture thumbtacked over his bed and everything.

"Mr. Emerson," says the assistant principal, who is bald except for a strip of hair that runs from ear to ear like a collar. "I'm glad you accompanied your friend Antonia here. But I'm afraid our business is with her. Would you mind waiting outside, young man?"

"No," Harrison says. Harrison is still staring at Just Carol. She's wearing dozens of bracelets that jangle every time she moves, earrings that look like the mobiles they put over baby cribs, and a bright gauze dress. She looks as if she is on her way to Hawaii.

"Now," Mr. Borgdorf says once the door is closed behind Harrison. "Miss Samberson says—"

"Who's that?" I ask.

"Carol." The assistant principal clears his throat as if saying her name plain like this gives him phlegm.

"Carol here says you've been telling people you're adopted . . . that your real parents are going to come and take you away to your real life. And, frankly, she is worried that something is going on." He glances at my mom. "At home."

I stare at Just Carol. My face feels hot, as if I have a fever. How could she have blabbed something like this?

"So," Mr. Borgdorf continues, "we thought we'd have a little talk here today and straighten this all out."

"Just tell me what to say so I can get out of here," I mutter, looking at the ceiling. One of the white panels is missing and there is brown paper underneath. Aren't you supposed to build buildings out of something more substantial than paper?

"Antonia," my mother's voice shoots out, as if it has been gathering force until now. "Don't play your games with me. You're not adopted and you know it."

"Fine. I'm not adopted. Can I leave now?"

"Look, Ant . . ." Just Carol leans forward in her chair. "I don't want to embarrass you, but I am concerned. It seems as if you're disturbed about something. I wanted to try to understand here. I thought we could all sit down and work it out."

"Butt out," I say without looking at her.

"Antonia!" my mom and Mr. Borgdorf call out in unison, then Mr. Borgdorf takes over. "I expect you to conduct yourself in an appropriate manner, young lady, with courteous and respectful language, otherwise I will put you on probation, on the spot. Consider yourself warned."

"Maybe you'd rather I hadn't brought this to the attention of Mr. Borgdorf," Just Carol says. "But I thought there was a problem that needed to be addressed. And I still believe that. Why is it you think you're adopted?"

"Because I am, that's all," I say, looking around for a window. It's twice as hot in this office as it is outside. How can Mr. Borgdorf stand to sit in here all day without a window?

"But there must be some reason you think this."

They are all staring at me. I know I'm not going anywhere unless I say something. "I don't look like my sisters. And I certainly don't act like them, because I never would behave as stupid as they do. And I wasn't named after a queen of England, like Your Highness Elizabeth and Katherine the Great."

"Antonia, you were named after your uncle Anthony. You know that," my mother says.

"Mrs. MacPherson, your daughter is unhappy. I don't think she feels a part of her family. Kids don't make up stories for no reason," Just Carol says.

"I didn't make it up," I say.

"Look, you don't know Antonia. She has a strange way of looking at things. She carries everything to the nth degree, and lying is a problem we've had over and over again. But we're working on it, aren't we,

Antonia?" My mother flashes her fake smile. "I appreciate your concern, truly I do, but I don't think this is the way to handle this."

"What about your dad?" Just Carol persists. "Is he your real father?"

"No," I say, speaking to the floor. "I have a whole other family. Only Pistachio is real. He's my real dog. When my real parents come, he's going with me."

My mother sighs. "I think we're giving her too much attention for this. It sends the wrong signal—"

"Bear with me a minute, Mrs. MacPherson," Just Carol says, motioning her hands like my mom should stop.

"Is this some new kind of teaching method?" my mother whispers to Mr. Borgdorf. Her foot is swinging back and forth.

"Miss Samberson." Mr. Borgdorf says her name like it is a complete sentence. "Step outside for a minute. I want to have a word with you." He shoots an embarrassed little smile in my mom's direction.

Great. The last thing I want is to be cooped up in a hot room with my mother. I scoot my chair away from her.

"Antonia, I just don't understand you. Do you want to humiliate me? Is that your purpose here?"

I look up. What would happen if I poked a hole in the paper where the ceiling panel is missing? What would come out?

"You weren't adopted."

I shrug. "That's what you always say."

"Because it's the truth," my mother says, taking a

tissue out of her sleeve and dabbing at her face. Her makeup is melting off. I can see a square patch on her forehead where her Kleenex has wiped it clean. "You know, I just don't understand you. I never have had a moment's worry with Elizabeth or Kate, either. But you, you're like some kind of . . . some kind of . . ."

"See," I whisper as Just Carol and the assistant principal come back, "you don't think I'm your real daughter, either."

Mr. Borgdorf's wide lips are pressed together. A sweat bead drops off his nose.

Just Carol sucks her cheeks in and organizes her jangly bracelets so the fronts are all going the same way.

"Now," the assistant principal says, "I think this has been a productive discussion for everyone. And I'm sure this is a situation you can work out at home, Mrs. MacPherson. And as for you, young lady . . . do you know the story of the boy who cried wolf?"

I nod.

"I think it would be instructive for you to relay that story to all of us here."

I run my tongue over my teeth. "Some kid pretended he saw a wolf a bunch of times, and everyone came to help him. Then when he really saw the wolf, they all thought he was kidding and they didn't come, and the wolf ate him."

"That's right. And what do you think the boy learned?" Mr. Borgdorf asks.

"He didn't learn anything. He's dead."

Mr. Borgdorf's eyes flash angry. His lips roll in.

"Fair enough. But why? What was the mistake he made?"

I blow my hair off my forehead and consider this question. "He was stupid. He shouldn't have expected anyone to help in the first place. He should have handled the wolf by himself. That's what I would have done."

2
HARRISON EMERSON

When the bus drops me and Harrison off, my little sister, Kate, is waiting for us. Kate looks like the kind of kid they show eating chocolate pudding on TV. She is small, even for a third grader, and she has blond curly hair and lots of freckles. She looks like my mom and my older sister, Your Highness Elizabeth. "Three peas in a pod," my father always says. "And one brown acorn." That's me. I have thick, straight dark hair and skin the color of a brown paper grocery bag. I don't look like anybody, except for my real parents, of course. I look exactly like them.

"Boy, are you in trouble," Kate says.

I stand on the curb looking back at the bus, wondering if it is too late for Harrison and me to get back on. The bus driver's big hand reaches for the silver door handle. The door slaps closed and the bus pulls back on the road, blowing stinky black smoke out the tailpipe.

"This is news?" I ask, cocking my head toward Harrison.

When Your Highness Elizabeth isn't around, Kate

spends her time watching me so she can report back to my mother. Sometimes she takes notes so she won't forget one single thing. I think Kate is going to be a bill collector when she grows up. She doesn't look like one, though, which is why she'll be so good at it.

"She lost a whole half-day at Barbara and Barbara's and she called Dad *at work,*" Kate says. We are walking now, and I hear coins jingle in her shoe. Kate always keeps change in there. She says it's the only safe place, because no one will ever think of stealing money from your shoe. The only problem is it sounds so loud when she walks that if someone did want to steal her money, they'd know right where to look.

"Big deal," I say, although this *is* a big deal. My mother works part-time as a bookkeeper for two interior designers named Barbara and she doesn't like to miss. And my father HATES to be called at work. I don't know why he hates this so much. It's not like he's a surgeon who will forget to put somebody's organs back if he gets a call in the middle of an operation. He works for an insurance company. What's so important about that?

"Life insurance is essential," Kate says. She half skips to keep up with us. "I'm thinking of buying some. You can make a lot of money with life insurance," she tells Harrison.

"Only problem is you got to die first," I say, kicking a dirt clod, which dissolves into a pile of dirt.

"You do not," she says.

"Yes, you do," I say.

"That doesn't make any sense at all, Antonia. Why would anyone want it then?" Kate says, her hands on her hips. Her chin poked out.

"Antonia Jane MacPherson, you're grounded! You come in here right this minute!" My mother's head bobs out the front door.

"Oh, man! She's home *already*?"

Kate nods. Her small face is very serious.

"I better go home," Harrison says. He scratches his neck under the collar of his T-shirt and takes a giant step backward. His arm is swinging back and forth, back and forth. He doesn't like being around my mom when she's mad at me, which is most of the time.

"Wait," I say to Harrison, grabbing his bony arm.

"Kate, will you walk Pistachio?" I ask.

"How much?"

I reach in my pocket to see what I have. "Eleven cents."

"Five dollars," Kate says.

"Are you nuts?" I sigh and look at Harrison, then I pull my ear twice. This is our secret sign. It means go around the back way. Harrison looks uncomfortable, as if he wishes I hadn't done that.

"Antonia," my mother yells. "I said right now. Harrison, you'll have to go home."

"Rats, Harrison!" I say, loud enough for my mom to hear. "You have to go home."

"Okay, I guess I'll go home now," Harrison says in a really fake voice. This is one problem with Harrison. He is a lousy liar.

Once I get to my room, Harrison will climb the

trellis in the backyard and come in the second-floor hall window. Harrison is good at getting in places. That's because his dad is always locking them out and sending Harrison in through the window to unlock the door.

"Bye, Harrison," Kate says. Kate kind of likes Harrison, though she would never admit it because Your Highness Elizabeth thinks Harrison is gross. He smells like a salami sandwich, Elizabeth always says.

Harrison smiles. Harrison likes everybody, whether they like him or not. He is even nice to people who make fun of him. This makes me sick. I think it's a basic rule of life never to be nice to people who make fun of you.

"Pistachio puked in your room," Kate says after Harrison disappears behind the Deetermans' garage. "It's yellow and it stinks worse than you know what."

"Better watch out, I'll tell Mom you said a nasty," I whisper.

"I did not! But even if I did, she'd never believe you, anyway. She never believes anything you say," Kate says. She seems proud of this.

I snort.

"Get a move on, Antonia," my mother bellows from the front door. "You go right up to your room and you stay there. You are not to leave this house, even to walk Pistachio."

"You always do that. It's not fair. Why should he get punished? What did he do?"

"Don't start with me, young lady. I have had it up to here with you." She touches her forehead, as if the floodwater has reached that high. "I don't want to hear one more word out of you," she says, then she goes back inside.

"$4.75 to walk him and that's my final offer," Kate whispers. Kate gets all her cash off me. She can never squeeze money out of Elizabeth because Elizabeth never gets in trouble. Maybe Kate will be a bail bondsman when she grows up. She would be good at that, too.

"I don't have $4.75."

"Yes, you do," Kate says. "It's in your bottom drawer."

"God, do you search my room, too?" I shove her out of the way so I can shortcut through the kitchen and score a handful of cookies without her telling my mother. It works. She stops to record my bad behavior in her spiral notebook. I make off with an entire package of Oreos and hurry up the stairs to my room.

My room is tiny. It was supposed to be the laundry room, but Elizabeth convinced my mom she'd get head lice from rooming with me, so they put the washer and dryer in the garage and I got my own room. The only problem is my room doesn't have a window, but it has a sink and that's almost as good.

"Hey, Tashi, hey, little guy," I say to my brown scruffy-haired dog, who is curled up asleep in my pajamas. Pistachio is tiny. He looks like a guinea pig, but he is a dog. He is old and he smells ripe.

Pistachio gets up when he sees me and twists his little body back and forth. He used to wait for me downstairs, then leap up and paw wildly at the air when I came home. But now, it's hard for him to stand up. He walks as if his legs don't bend, and his fur used to be white around his face, but now it's yellow. No matter how hard I scrub, I can't get it clean.

He makes my room stink, too. Especially if he has puked. Today I smell the nasty stink of food that's come back up. I look for puke puddles. There are two on my bedspread and one on the rug. Yuck. I carry Pistachio to the laundry basket and get him settled in a nest of dirty socks. Then I strip my bed and go downstairs for new sheets and rug cleaner. My mother is in the kitchen, but I know she won't yell at me for this. As far as she is concerned, even mass murderers should be allowed to clean their rooms.

I go straight for the cleaning cupboard so she'll know what I am doing, and I keep quiet. My mom and I get along fine when I keep my mouth shut, but the second I say so much as "Hello" I get in trouble. If I were a mute, it would be much better.

"I'm going to pick up Elizabeth at ballet class. If Kate tells me you've been out of this house"—my mother drums her fingers on the counter—"Pistachio will sleep outside."

I look down at my mom's ankle. If I were a dog, I'd bite her. I smile to myself, thinking about this.

By the time I get back to my room, Harrison is there, balancing an Oreo on his nose. We listen while the garage door goes up, *tchinka-tchinka-tchinka squeareak*. It sounds as if it won't make it up or down again, which is the way this whole house is. It's painted this weird color on the outside—like when you mess up in art class and your paints run together in one greenish brownish mess. And nothing inside the house works very well. The washing machine overflows, the cupboard doors are always falling off, and the garbage disposal sounds like it's grinding up body parts.

This is a temporary house. "A rental," my mom calls it. The garage is filled with boxes my mother won't unpack until we "get a place of our own." My parents have never bought a house, but that is always the plan once we get settled. The thing is we never do get settled. We always just move again. I have moved thirteen times in my life. This is actually the longest we've ever lived anywhere. We've been in the house just off the road Sarah's Road in the town of Sarah's Road for two years. I plan on staying here forever, too, because I like Sarah's Road, even if it is a silly name for a city. And because this is where Harrison lives.

I look at Harrison scooping the white center out of the Oreo with his crooked front teeth and I feel happy. Before Harrison, I had people I called friends, but they were just kids to eat lunch with. That's way different.

Harrison shakes his head and looks up at me through his wild hair. "Your dad home?"

I shake my head. "Friday."

"How come he's gone so much, anyway?"

"He's in charge of a bunch of sales offices and he has to visit them. And sometimes he opens new ones and hires people and trains them and stuff."

Harrison scratches his head all over, like he's

shampooing his hair. "I don't want a job like that. Think I could find a job drawing chickens?"

"Maybe, you know, the ones on the packages in the grocery store."

"Yuck." Harrison's face scrunches up. "Those are dead chickens. I don't want to draw dead chickens!" He shakes his head and looks at me as if I've just licked dirt.

"I'm sorry." I hand him the package of Oreos. He takes three. "I know what we can do. I'll get a job and then I'll buy all your chicken drawings. Every single one of them."

Harrison smiles. "Okay," he says. He carves the white out of another cookie. "That reminds me, are we going to do that report card thing again this semester?"

Last year Harrison and I switched report cards. Harrison cut the names off the top with a razor blade and a ruler. Then, I took home his report card, which was full of C's and D's and one A+ in art. And he took home my report card, which had all A's and B's except for one D- in Citizenship—up from an F in the fall.

"I dunno. You want to?" I ask.

"I still can't believe no one figured it out. Ours were a half inch shorter than everyone else's." He measures out a half inch with his thumb and forefinger and stares at it.

"I know, plus the signatures were wrong." I shake my head. "No one writes clearer than my mom. How could Cave Man have missed my mom's signature on *your* report card?"

"Do you think they'll be that stupid again?" Harrison is looking down now, picking the nubs off my blanket and putting them in a pile.

"Why not?"

Harrison's curly hair hangs in his eyes. He flicks the nub pile with his finger and it topples over. "Yeah, but I don't see what *you* get out of it. Are you sure your mom didn't get mad when she saw my grades?"

I shrug. "She's used to it. Besides, it makes your dad happy. Maybe he'll take us out for ice cream again. That was fun."

Harrison pulls the pills off the blanket and rolls them in his hand. He's forming some kind of blanket-lint creature. Harrison can make something out of anything. He shrugs. "Okay," he says.

"Good. Now let's get out of here." I pocket a few Oreos, grab Pistachio, and we sneak down the trellis to take him for a walk.

When we get to the sidewalk, I put Pistachio down, but he doesn't move. I hate when he gets stuck like this. "Come on, Tashi," I say, grabbing a leaf for him to sniff.

He sniffs a little, then takes a step forward. Once he gets started, he seems okay, like he remembers what he's supposed to do. He walks stiff legged over to the bushes and begins sniffing around. After a minute, he tries to lift his leg, but he wobbles so much on three legs, it looks as if he'll topple over. I want to tell him to pee another way.

"Guess what?" Harrison says as I hand him another Oreo. "I found out where Just Carol lives."

"Just Carol. Who cares about her? She's a worm. You can't trust her. I told you what she did. I still can't believe she told my mom and Mr. Borgdorf. . . ." I am just getting warmed up with my story when Harrison presses his hands over his ears. "Harrison? What?" I ask.

"Just Carol is not a worm. Just Carol is perfect."

"God, Harrison, whose side are you on, anyway?"

Harrison has his hands covering his ears again.

"Harrison?" I try to peel his fingers away from his head.

"I'm on your side. But don't be ugly about Just Carol."

"Okay, okay, I won't say anything bad about her. Man." I glare at him. I would get madder, but he looks as if he might cry. I hate when Harrison cries.

"Come on," I say, scooping up Pistachio. "Let's go to the yellow house."

The yellow house is on a street where the houses are all old-fashioned. Two German shepherds and one black Lab live there. I like the dogs and their pretty house with the swing on the porch and the kind of white arch people get married under. This is the type of house my real parents would live in.

I change my mind about who my real parents are at least once a week. I have a book where I write down my notes about this. There are a lot of names in it, but they are mostly crossed out. I keep it in a hole in the lining of my raincoat, along with another book that has photos of me and things I've written and pictures I've drawn and stuff. The second book is for my real parents. It will help them know about the parts of my life they haven't been here to see.

We are at the yellow house now, so I put Pistachio down. Right away his tail goes straight in the air and he begins barking his ferocious bark. Pistachio weighs six pounds, but something in his brain tells him he is a 150-pound killer dog. Nothing perks him up like picking a fight with a dog ten times his size. Harrison's father says some wires in his brain are crossed and he thinks he is a tiger.

As soon as he starts barking, the German shepherds come running to the chain-link fence. They stand on their hind legs and try to get at Pistachio. The fence shakes. Their lips curl back. The German shepherds are barking so loud, it hurts my ears. They look mean, but not the Lab. She gets scared and lies on her back with her legs straight up.

"One down, Pistachio! Good dog," I say. This seems to please him and he takes a rest. The German shepherds get tired of barking, too, and all the dogs sit down.

Harrison takes out his chicken drawing, which I know he has been dying to finish. He rummages through his pockets looking for a pencil. Harrison has ten or twelve pockets in his pants, so looking for a pencil can take a long time. I watch while he goes through pocket by pocket. He finally finds a No. 2 in his zipper pocket. It's a little stub with bite marks all around. Harrison likes his pencils already broken in.

We sit down with our backs against the chain link and Harrison starts drawing. I like to watch him draw. He is so patient about it, as if he knows exactly where he's going and how to get there. He doesn't get frustrated the way I do. I've never seen him scrunch his paper up and toss it on the floor.

He doesn't get very far today, though, before we hear the beep-beep of Harrison's father's bakery truck. The truck is an old-fashioned van that looks like a cartoon car. Harrison's father owns a bakery and this is one of the delivery trucks.

"Well, hello, fancy meeting you here," Harrison's father says. Harrison and his dad never have a set meeting time or place. His dad just drives around Sarah's Road until he finds Harrison. Only a dad would do that. Moms would make sure you have a time and a place to meet. But Harrison doesn't have a mom. She died when he was four. He never talks about her, either, and the way he steers way around the subject, I know better than to ask. Once, Mr. Emerson told me Mrs. Emerson was an artist. That is all I know about her.

"Hi, Dad," Harrison says.

"Hello, Harrison, hello, Ant. How are you and that ferocious tiger dog doing?"

This makes me smile, even though he says it almost every time he sees me.

"Hey, Dad," Harrison says. "Could Ant spend the night tonight?"

"That okay with your mom, Ant?" Mr. Emerson asks. He has the same goofy smile Harrison does. And the same wildly curly hair, though he is losing some of his on top.

I always plan to lie to this question, but when it comes time, I never can. I have the feeling that no matter how many times I lie to Mr. Emerson, he'll still believe me. And because of this, I have trouble telling him anything but the truth. My mom is just the opposite. She never believes me, so it doesn't matter what I tell her. I grab a dandelion and flick it with my thumb. "No," I say.

My mom has forbidden me from ever going to Harrison's house. This is because last month my mother picked me up there and she saw Harrison's chicken walk in using the doggy door. "What kind of people have chicken droppings in their house?" she said. I tried to tell her they only let the chicken in the kitchen. Plus, Harrison trained him to use a kitty litter box, which the vet said was impossible, but Harrison did it anyway. But none of this matters to my mom.

Harrison's father makes a sound as if he's sorry. "Oh, well, Ant, my girl. Maybe the weekend." He pats my head awkwardly. "Okay, son, time to pack up and go. I've got 800 pounds of flour and sugar coming crack of dawn tomorrow and still no space for it. So you say good-bye to Ant here and we'll be on our way."

"Bye, Harrison," I say as he jumps into the cab of the old van.

Harrison smiles at me. One side of his mouth curls up more than the other and he has a dimple in his left cheek. I love this about him.

I stand and watch them drive past the bank of mailboxes, across the bridge, and around the corner onto

Sarah's Road. I watch until I can't see them anymore. Then I pick up Pistachio and walk home.

My mom is in the living room when I get there. I see her curly blond hair through the window. She is sitting on the couch watching Elizabeth show Kate the steps she learned in ballet class. I wonder if Kate has noticed I am gone. I wonder if my mom has looked to see if I am in my room. The way they are acting, I don't think they have. I should be happy about this, but I am sad.

3
LITTLE BROWN ACORN

Today is the big day. My dad's coming home from Atlanta. He's been there for six weeks. My sisters and my mom are locked in the bathroom getting ready for him. When they come out, Your Highness Elizabeth and Kate are wearing matching tutus with sparkles glued to the bushy ends and sequined tiaras. My mother has made up Elizabeth's and Kate's faces so they look like plastic dolls. They are planning to perform a show for my dad. They always do this. They set up the living room to look like a theater, with big boxes of popcorn and a cardboard marquee. Then they hide behind the living-room drapes and my mom pulls the cord and they do a ballet dance. When they are done, they say, "Ta-da," and my father and mother give them a standing ovation.

When I was little, I used to do this, too. That was when I went to ballet class with Your Highness Elizabeth. But now I won't because it's stupid and I would rather be outside with Harrison and Pistachio. My mother says I am a quitter. But I'm not a quitter, I just don't feel like spending the day in front of a mirror worrying about whether my butt is sticking out.

Kate is taking ballet classes now, too. She is as good as Elizabeth. "It runs in the family," Miss Marion Margo, the dance teacher, says, forgetting all about me. Or maybe she hasn't forgotten. Maybe even strangers can tell that I am a part of another family entirely. Probably no one will be surprised when my real parents sweep into the picture. My real mother will be wearing a flowered dress and no shoes. And my real father will have on jeans and chaps. My real father is very smart. He knows how to get water from a cactus when you are in the middle of the Mojave Desert. Plus, he is a cowboy, and cowboys never get a job somewhere else. They have to stay home and take care of their cattle. Maybe they go to a different range, but that is it.

"Aren't you going to at least wash your hair?" Your Highness Elizabeth asks as she bristles by the door of my room in her tutu. "Mom, look at her hair. It's disgusting." Elizabeth picks up a strand of my hair and drops it again, as if someone has told her it is contaminated.

"Of course, Your Highness . . . whatever you wish, Your Highness." I bow down low.

"See what she's like, Mom? See?"

"All right, enough, you two. I don't want any fights in front of your father. Antonia, you might think about putting on some clean clothes before you come down."

"Come down? How can I come down? I'm not allowed out of my room, remember?"

My mother takes a deep breath. I can tell she is thinking about calling me a smart mouth or a wiseacre, but she holds her tongue. She doesn't like to get angry right before my father comes home from a business trip. She wants everything to be perfect, like we are a family ordered from a catalog. "Well, if you want to watch the wonderful show your sisters have put together, you're welcome to," she says.

"Spare me," I say.

"Don't bother trying to be nice to her, Mom. She doesn't even know how to accept it," Elizabeth says as she watches herself in the hall mirror. She is standing up straight, trying to make her neck extra long. She says ballerinas all have very long necks. Hers is kind of squatty, so she is trying to stretch it.

"Oh no! My tiara!" Kate cries. Kate's sequined tiara is slipping off and her curly hair is coming unpinned. Her whole face is red and she is bawling, open-mouthed like a three-year-old. I can't believe her. Where is her spiral notebook? Where are the coins she carries in her shoe? Has she forgotten all about blackmail? I hate the way she turns into a mini Elizabeth when Elizabeth and my mother are around. One Your Highness is bad enough.

"Kate," I whisper when she walks by, but she pretends not to hear me. When Elizabeth is paying attention to her, she forgets all about me.

I close the door. Not a slam, but loud. Then I sit on my bed, wondering whether my mother will come back and ask me to put on a dress and come downstairs. I plan my speech about how there is no way I'm going to do this. Then, I wait. But there is no sound of creaking stairs. All the footsteps stay away.

I take out the book I'm making for my real parents and I begin writing a letter to my real mom.

Dear Real Mom,

This is what I would like to happen. I would like you and my real dad to come RIGHT NOW. Then first thing after you get here, you should tell my supposed mom (her name is Evelyn MacPherson) about how I'm your daughter and I'm very special and you are just wild about me. I can't wait to see her face when you say this. Maybe you could tell her how I am much smarter than Elizabeth and Kate and you don't understand how come she hasn't figured this out. And you might mention that Elizabeth's neck is unusually short and squatty and you don't see how anyone could be a ballerina with a short, squatty neck like that.

Then, when you see my supposed dad (his name is Don MacPherson), you can say you know he has a lot of problems at work and you are sorry. And if you have any extra money, maybe you can give it to him. Then you can shake hands and say "Good-bye," and I will kick off my shoes and get on the pinto horse you brought for me, and me and Pistachio will ride away with you and my real dad.

Love,
Ant and Pistachio
P.S. I hope you live near Harrison. Do you?

• • •

Pistachio snuggles next to me on my bed. He licks my hand. His tongue is hot, like it's come from a furnace. I am thinking that I will take him back to the vet tomorrow, when I hear the *tchinka-tchinka-tchinka squereak* of the garage door. I run to the hall window to look out. It's my father all right. I feel excited to see him, though that is not something I plan to tell him or anyone else.

When I was little, I used to love my father, but now I don't know. He liked me better when I was little and stupid—when I thought every idea he came up with was the greatest thing. He doesn't want a daughter. He wants a fan. Kate and Elizabeth are his fans now. I am not.

My father parks his car half in the garage and half out of it. He always parks this way, I don't know why.

"He's here! He's here!" my sisters yell. For a second, I think about yelling this, too, and running down the stairs to meet him. I imagine him putting his arms around me and hugging me in his big hug way.

Elizabeth and Kate bolt outside in their tights and tutus. Kate is jumping up and down. Elizabeth must have forgotten she is too grown-up for this, because she is jumping up and down, too. Now my dad is carrying Elizabeth under one arm and Kate under the other. He walks pitched forward like his shoulders can't wait for his legs to catch up. He lets my sisters down and sweeps my mother off her feet, like the leading men in the old movies. My father is tall and blond, and he looks almost as handsome as an actor. Not the leading guy, though. The leading guy's brother.

They are inside now. I strain to hear what they're saying. Elizabeth and Kate are both talking at once, telling my dad how they are doing in school. "One at a time," my mother says. I look at my watch, wondering how long it will take for him to ask about me. My sisters blabber on about ballet class and their friends and the show they can't wait to perform. Then my mother gets her turn. She tells him about a lady she met at Barbara and Barbara's who got her house repossessed. She is pretending to sound sorry, but her voice is happy, like when she gets the right answer on *Who Wants to Be a Millionaire.*

"Where's Antonia?" my father asks when my mother takes a breath. I look at my watch. Eleven minutes, thirty-three seconds.

"Where do you think?" my mother answers.

My father takes the steps two at a time. He always does this. I don't know if it is because he's tall or always in a hurry. He knocks on my door. *Rat-a-tat-tat,* even the knock is a celebration.

I put my head against the little ball of Pistachio and say nothing.

"Little Brown Acorn, are you in there?"

I'm quiet. I blink the tears back.

My father knocks again. When I don't answer, he opens the door a crack. "Antonia, are you okay?"

"Sure," I say. "I'm fine. I'm seeing to Pistachio is all. He's sick."

"Oh," he says, glancing down at Pistachio as if he has forgotten I have a dog. "You don't want to come down and welcome your dad home?"

I think about telling him that he is not my real dad, so there's no sense in me going through this nonsense about welcoming him home. But I don't. "I can't leave," I say. "Pistachio needs me."

He blows air out of his nose and bites his bottom lip, the way he does when he's annoyed. This is not the way things are supposed to go when he comes home. There is supposed to be a show and then he is supposed to give out presents and then we are supposed to eat a special dinner.

"I have a present with your name on it," he says. "I guess I'll have to give it to Elizabeth." I can see by the way he says this that he is sure this will make me come around. It has worked before.

"I guess so," I say. I wonder what he has brought this time. Once he gave us Mexican blouses. Another time, it was wooden shoes. The thing is he never travels to Mexico or Holland, he always goes to places like Cleveland or Omaha or St. Louis, so I am not sure how he gets those gifts, but he does. I hope he will suggest I bring Pistachio downstairs. I think about telling him I will come down if I can bring Tashi.

We are both quiet a long time. I smell the lasagna my mother is cooking. It smells like tomatoes and garlic and fried onions. My mother makes great lasagna. It's the only thing she doesn't make from a box.

I try to open my mouth to ask if Pistachio can come downstairs with me, but I am too slow. "Suit yourself, Antonia," he says, and walks out of my room, closing the door between us.

I jump up and open it again. "My name is Ant."

He stops at the stairs and shakes his head without even looking at me. "Ants ruin a picnic, Antonia," he says, and then he is gone.

The tears are hot in my eyes. It's safe to let them fall. I've hurt his feelings, he won't be back. I creep out into the hall and strain to hear what is going on downstairs.

"What happened?" my mom asks.

"She says Pistachio is sick and he needs her. I'm gone for six weeks and she doesn't even come down to say hello. She doesn't need anybody, does she?"

4
PISTACHIO

All weekend I've been watching Pistachio, trying to figure out what to do. He is so tired, he doesn't do anything but sleep and stand at my door as if he wants to go out. But when I take him out he wants to go in. In. Out. In. Out. He is all confused, and he can't seem to get comfortable. His brown eyes are dull, as if even the simplest decision is too much for him. He looks up at me like can't I do something to make him feel better?

I don't know how to help. I've taken him to the clinic twice in the last few weeks, but they don't seem to know what's the matter. "A blander diet," the vet with the chunky blond braid said, and then she gave me this special food that's a funny yellow color and smells like vitamins. Tashi won't touch it. The vet with the shaky hands gave him a shot. That didn't help, either. Then I tried the rice and cottage cheese diet, and my mom went nuts. "Why on earth are you feeding cottage cheese to a dog?" she asked. "Do you know how much it costs?" Cottage cheese is nothing compared to what a visit to the doggy doctor costs. But my mom doesn't know I've been going there.

The problem is my mom hates dogs. So does my dad. It's pretty amazing that we even have a dog. What happened was right after we moved to Sarah's Road, my father was supposed to open an insurance office in Toledo. My dad wanted this really good insurance agent named Irene to move from Indiana to Ohio so she could run the office. But Irene wouldn't go, on account of she had three dogs and landlords don't like to rent to you if you have pets. But my dad wanted her really bad, so on one of his trips to Toledo, he found her a cute house to rent where the landlord said it was okay to have three dogs. Only problem was by moving day, Irene didn't have three dogs. She had four.

Apparently a part-Chihuahua mutt followed Irene home from the park and Irene had not been able to find his owner. So my father called the landlord in Toledo to see if he would allow four dogs, but the guy said forget it, four are too many.

By then, my father needed Irene even worse than before because the office was supposed to open in two weeks, so he promised he'd find a home for the tiny half-Chihuahua dog Irene called Pistachio. That night Pistachio came to our house on a "strictly temporary basis," and the next day my mom put up Free Dog signs with our phone number on little pull tabs. Shortly after that all those signs "mysteriously disappeared." I must have missed some, though, because one lady did call. Luckily, I answered the phone, and by the time I got through telling her all of Pistachio's bad habits—those he has and those he might someday develop—she said, "No, thank you."

Then my mom got mad at my dad. She said she was going to take *that dog* to the pound. But my dad said he promised Irene he wouldn't do that. Then I swore for the hundredth time I would clean up after Pistachio and keep him out of my mom's sight. She wouldn't even know we had a dog. But my mom said no. Every day I'd ask and every day she'd say no. After a few weeks I finally figured out my mom didn't have any idea what to do with Pistachio and if I just kept quiet, he could stay.

The problem is she won't spend money on him. She buys dog food, but that's it. This is why when I take him to the vet, I get a temporary case of dyslexia. I put all the right numbers and all the right letters on the forms, I just mix up the order quite a bit. I have to. The last time the vet cost $128. Who has that kind of money?

This time I'm going to need her to pay, though, because she's going to have to drive me. None of the vet clinics in Sarah's Road are open on Sunday nights, which is the stupidest thing in the world. How are dogs supposed to know to get sick during business hours? There is only one vet clinic open all night, but it's an hour's drive away. My dad isn't home right now, neither are Harrison and Mr. Emerson. I try to think of what I can say to my mom to get her to take Tashi to the vet.

I walk downstairs with Pistachio tucked in the crook of my arm. My mom is watching *Antiques*

Roadshow with Kate. My mom and Kate love this show. They get all excited when somebody has an old Egyptian urn they think is worth $5 and it turns out to be worth $50,000. "Hah, I knew it. Did you know it? I knew it," they tell the TV.

"Mom?"

My mom turns away from the screen. "Antonia, you know perfectly well that dog is not allowed in the living room."

I step back off the rug onto the linoleum in the entranceway.

"Mom, would you come out to the kitchen? I need you to look at Pistachio." My mother sighs. She picks up her empty glass and follows me through the push door.

"Mom, he's really sick. We have to do something!"

My mother sets her glass on the counter and gets a bottle of lemon seltzer out of the refrigerator. "Antonia, he's a dog. What am I supposed to tell you?"

"Yeah, and he's sick. Can't you see?"

She groans, pours her seltzer, and stands with her glass in her hand. We both look at Pistachio.

"His nose is hot. He's hot all over. He's not eating. Look, here's a Milk-Bone." I put him down on the floor. "He loves Milk-Bones. But he won't even sniff it. He doesn't even get up when I come in now. He's not like this normally, Mom. He's not!"

Elizabeth floats in and pulls open the refrigerator. She gets some apple juice and pours it in her favorite pink cup. She looks down at Pistachio. "He does look sick, Mom. And if he dies in this house it will be the grossest thing. There will be maggots and worms. It will smell awful. The whole house will be contaminated. I can't live in a house with a dead dog in it. Not even 409 can help that."

"Shut up! Why do you have to be so mean?" I ask.

Elizabeth ignores me. "Just call the animal-control people. They'll take him." She picks up her pink cup and walks out of the kitchen.

"So," my mom says slowly. "What is it you want from me, Antonia?" My mother raises one eyebrow.

"We've got to take him to the vet, Mom."

"Antonia, for God's sake . . ."

"If you were me, how would you get you to take Pistachio to the vet?"

"If I were you, I'd forget it. We don't have that kind of money. I spent $200 on the vet last time. Remember that? That was two weeks' worth of groceries. I can't be spending that kind of money every time your dog has a little headache." My mom puts rice crackers on a plate and pushes the kitchen door open with her foot. I follow her.

"What if we were the richest people in the world, would you pay to take Pistachio to the vet then?"

"That's a ridiculous question, Antonia."

I stop at the metal bar that marks the beginning of the rug. I raise my voice so she'll hear me over the TV. "What if I did double chores, plus the laundry, plus the dishes and the weeding and the sweeping up, would you do it then?"

"If you did the laundry, Antonia, our clothes would turn blue. If you swept the floor, your sweeping would make the place twice as dirty. And besides that, no means no! What part of no don't you understand?" Mrs. MacPherson saw this on a mug a few months ago and ever since then it's been her favorite saying. She thinks she's clever every time she says it.

"Look, Mom! Look!" I hold Pistachio up. "He's suffering. It's our responsibility to take care of him. It is." I wish I could make her see how sick he is. The way he feels heavier to hold now, like dead weight, and he barely lifts up his head. You have to really know Pistachio to understand how un-Pistachio-like he is being.

My mom moves the couch pillow behind her back. "He's old, Antonia. I'm sorry about that. I am. But there's nothing a vet can do about it. Dogs get old. They die. Cats get old. They die. People get old and die, too. You know that."

I cover Pistachio's ears. "'Jingle bells, jingle bells, jingle all the way,'" I sing in his ear so he can't hear what my mom's saying.

"Antonia, if he's still sick in a few days, we'll talk about going to the vet, okay?" She takes a bite of her rice cracker and turns back to the TV.

"Oh, great, and what if he dies in the meantime?"

"Don't be so dramatic."

"Well, you just said he was old and he was going to die."

"Antonia, I'm not taking that dog to the vet tonight. On Wednesday, if he's still sick, we'll talk about it again."

"When you get old and sick," I whisper, "and you

need to go to the doctor, I'll remember this. Let's wait a few days and see if you die first, I'll say."

Luckily, my mom and Kate don't hear me.

"Mom." I walk right into the living room and hold Pistachio's little body out at her.

"Antonia, get that dog out of the living room! I have half a mind to take him to the pound right this minute! And what are you doing down here, anyway? You're still grounded!"

Dear Real Mom,

Well, this confirms it. Mrs. MacPherson is the meanest person in the whole world. And I know for sure I am not the daughter of someone this mean. In fact, I'm not related to her in any way, and I know I wasn't inside her belly or attached to her by any umbilical cord, either. Elizabeth and Kate probably were because they are mean, too. But not me. If I was inside my mom's belly, I held my breath the whole time!

Love,

Ant and Pistachio

When I hear my father come home, I head downstairs. It's very late now and the chances of getting him in the car at eleven at night for any reason short of a neighborhood evacuation are slim. But I'm afraid tomorrow will be too late. What if Pistachio dies? This is too horrible to imagine. I'll stay up all night and protect him, that's what I'll do. Only my bed is looking soft and warm right now and my pillow is calling me. What if I fall asleep?

My mom and dad are in the living room talking. I open my mouth to say my dad's name, but something about the tone of his voice makes me close it again. "I'm sick of this, Evelyn," he says. "The last thing I want to do is get on an airplane and fly to Atlanta tomorrow, believe me. But do you think Dave cares about that?" My dad makes a noise like he is pretend spitting. "All he cares about are the numbers. And frankly, with the job market right now, I can get a new job"—my father snaps his fingers—"like that. I got headhunters calling me every week. I don't have to put up with this."

Uh-oh. Not again. Please not again. My stomach starts to churn. This always happens. At first, my dad is happy with his new job and everything is GREAT. Then, his boss starts to bug him or the people he works with or the way the computers are set up or how the sales territories are divided, and he gets UN-HAPPY and then he CAN'T STAND IT, and then he quits. And we move somewhere else and the whole thing starts all over again.

"But you're not going to quit tomorrow," my mother says, her voice uncertain. My mom is sitting on the couch. Her back is to me. My father is in his chair. I am in his line of vision, but it's dark and there's only one light turned on, plus my dad is so caught up in what he's saying, he hasn't noticed me yet.

"I do the work, Dave gets the credit. I was in a meeting with all the top guys on Friday: Joe Marcioni, Nancy Rapier, Robert Cordoba, everyone. And there's Dave reporting the numbers on the Albuquerque office without even mentioning me. He acts like—"

"But we're not going to move! You said we were going to stay here!" I blurt out. I hadn't planned on saying this. My mouth decided on its own.

My father jumps. "What are you doing down here?" he asks.

"Antonia, you know how I feel about eavesdropping," my mother says. She is turned around. Her hand is resting on the back of the couch.

"I wasn't eavesdropping. I was standing right out in the open. You just didn't see me."

"Well, why didn't you say something?" my mother asks.

"*Dad*, are we?" I look hard at him.

"No, honey, we're not. I'm just talking to your mom, that's all. What did you come down here for?"

"Pistachio is sick and we have to take him to the vet."

"Antonia, for God's sake! You're like a broken record about that dog," my mother says. She takes a sip of wine.

"Not you, Mom. I'm asking Dad. Irene would want us to, you know. We owe it to her. If Pistachio dies, you're going to need to tell Irene. That would really upset her. She might quit working for you and everything."

"Antonia, your mother is right. Let's give the dog a few days, then see how he is. Besides, it's eleven o'clock on a Sunday night. No animal doctor is going to be working—"

"Yes, there is. There's an all-night clinic in Terra Linda. I saw it in the Yellow Pages."

My father groans.

"You walked right into that one, Don." My mother laughs.

My dad rests his chin on the palm of his hand. "It's not going to happen, Antonia. I'm not driving to Terra Linda tonight."

"Dad, *please!*"

"You know, Antonia, I'm gone for six weeks and you don't even come out of your room to say hello. And then all of a sudden you need something from me and I'm supposed to rush out at eleven at night."

"He's sick, Dad. Punish me. Don't punish him!"

"I'm sorry, Antonia."

"Will you at least come see him?"

My father follows me up the stairs. I open the door of my room and pull the chain on the overhead light. Pistachio is curled in a ball on my pillow. He blinks his eyes and hides his head in his tail. The light is too bright.

"He's sleeping, Antonia."

"Pet him," I say.

My father gives me a funny look. "Does he bite?"

"God, Dad." I roll my eyes. I take his big soft hand and put it on Pistachio. "Pet him."

My dad pets in short stiff motions, as if he is stamping Pistachio with his hand.

"This is silly," my father says. He snorts and pulls his hand away. "Antonia, the dog looks fine. Go to sleep." He pulls the chain on my light and closes the door.

"Promise me you'll be okay," I tell Pistachio. I hold

the raspy side of his little paw and breathe in his warm smell like mud and raisins. "Swear to God, okay?"

Pistachio pulls his paw away and curls himself into a tighter little ball. I rest my ear by his nose and listen to his breathing. *Phuuu. Phuuu. Phuuu.* Even if I fall asleep like this, I'll be able to hear if anything is wrong and I will wake up right away.

5

THE VET

I'm sitting on a wooden planter outside the veterinarian's office waiting for them to open. I peek through the window. The office has wood walls and a busy design on the linoleum, probably so no one will notice when a dog pees on the floor. There's a bunch of animal pictures on the wall and a bench that runs along two sides of the room. On a table in the corner, there are magazines and a plastic heart all covered with fake spaghetti.

I'm wondering what the fake spaghetti is supposed to be, when the receptionist arrives. She has a long ponytail and she's eating a Pop-Tart. A fluffy white dog is following her. The dog is waiting, his eyes glued on the girl. He seems to know the last bite of Pop-Tart will be his. He is not on a leash. This is a good sign. It means this vet doesn't run what my dad calls "a tight ship."

I expect Pistachio to perk up when he sees the dog, but he doesn't seem to care. I tell the receptionist girl how sick Pistachio's been and how worried I am. She wipes red fruit filling from the corners of her mouth with the back of her hand. "Okay, leave him and I'll have the vet check him out when she gets in," she says. She doesn't ask anything about money. So far so good. I give her a backward address and phone number and tell her I will stop by after school to pick up Pistachio and find out what the vet says to do. The phone rings. The receptionist picks it up and nods at me as if everything has been squared away. I hand her Pistachio. He is whimpering pitifully, and my heart clutches up tight.

The receptionist puts her hand over the phone and gently strokes Pistachio's fur. "Don't worry. We'll take good care of him." She winks at me.

I feel a little better, but when I go outside, I hear Pistachio cry even louder, now that I'm gone. I put my hand in my pocket. It feels empty and light. I want to go back, but I know it's better not to. I don't want the vet to come and ask a lot of questions. Lying only works if you keep it short.

When I get to school it's already art class. Cave Man is teaching math to the other sixth-grade class and Just Carol is in our room, showing everyone how to make peacocks out of Styrofoam balls, fake feathers, and pipe cleaners. I don't like peacocks. They remind me of Your Highness Elizabeth—pretty and always showing off. Harrison likes this project, though. He is standing so close to Just Carol, she can hardly move her arms. He listens to Just Carol as if she were telling him survival information. But when he does his art projects, they don't turn out like hers. They turn out better.

I smile when I think of this because it reminds me of the first day I came to school in Sarah's Road. We had just moved here from Las Vegas, and, as usual, we moved in the middle of the school year, after everybody has already made friends. I don't think we've ever moved in the summer, the way other people do. Anyway, no one was expecting me, so there wasn't a seat in Mrs. Betterman's class. "Antonia, take the empty desk in the back for today," Mrs. Betterman said. "It's Harrison Emerson's seat, but he's out sick. His math book should be inside. Could you turn to page 209 and read us the definition of perimeter?" I opened Harrison's desk, pulled out his math book, and turned to page 209. Only there was no 209. Harrison had cut out pages 175 through 230 and replaced them with drawing paper covered with these amazing sketches of chickens—roosters, hens, baby chicks, close-up drawings of chicken feet, chicken beaks, chicken feathers—every chicken part was present and accounted for in Harrison Emerson's math book.

I've never really liked chickens, but these drawings were so beautiful, I changed my mind on the spot. I couldn't believe a fourth grader could draw like that and I wasn't about to get this person, whoever he was, busted. So I hit my forehead with my palm and I said, "Oh no! I forgot my glasses! I'm sorry, Mrs. Betterman. I can't read a word without my glasses!"

The next day when Harrison came back to school, the girl who sat beside him told him what I did. Harrison and me started being friends that day. And we have never stopped.

I get my Styrofoam ball and start sticking feathers in it. My hands are working, but my mind is back thinking about Pistachio. I worry about him all alone at the vet's.

"Ant? Ant? ANT?" Just Carol is calling my name. I blink my eyes. Uh-oh. She motions with her finger to follow her. I walk to the back of the room by a bulletin board filled with ocean animals cut out of bright construction paper colors. Harrison is right behind Just Carol. Maybe he needs more pipe cleaners, although it is more likely he wants to eavesdrop. "Did you call me on the phone on Friday?" Just Carol asks as she sorts the leftover pipe cleaners by color.

"Why would I call you?" I ask.

"I don't know, but every time I answered, whoever it was hung up."

"How do you know it was me?"

She shakes her head. Her dangly earrings tinkle. "I don't."

"Well, first off, I don't know your number. But even if I did, I'd never call you. I don't even like you."

Just Carol's face gets pale. I feel a pain as if something is squishing my toe. Harrison is stomping my foot.

"Look, I know you're angry with me," Just Carol says. Her eyes are green like algae and full of feeling. "And I can't say I blame you. If I were you, I'd be angry, too. That discussion in Mr. Borgdorf's office did not turn out the way I planned it. I thought I was helping, but the whole thing blew up in my face. And now I'm sorry I said anything at all."

I look away, surprised. I've heard teachers apologize to right a wrong before, but never because they felt bad. Almost never, anyway. Once we had a substitute who apologized all the time, but Mr. Borgdorf asked her to leave because he said we "walked all over her."

But this is different. Just Carol isn't usually like this. She sends kids to the office all the time. In fact, when Just Carol is in a bad mood, nobody dares cross her. "I don't have to put up with this," she'll say for something little like hogging the glitter, and then whoever it is will be sent to the other sixth-grade class to do math with Cave Man twice that day.

"I want to try to make it up to you," Just Carol continues, fussing with her bracelets. "It seems as if you and Harrison really love animals." I look over at Harrison. His whole face is glowing. "So I was wondering if you would like to be a part of Zoo Teens." Even before she finishes saying this, Harrison begins nodding.

I have no idea what Zoo Teens are, but I am very pleased to be asked to be a teen anything.

"What do they do?" I ask.

"It's a program on Saturdays where kids get to help the keepers take care of the zoo animals."

"Like lions and bears and elephants?"

"Like lions and bears and elephants, yes."

"Would I get to brush them and ride them?"

"No. They're wild animals. We feed them, clean the night houses and the exhibit areas, and help with enrichment."

"What's that?"

"Enrichment? It's making their lives more fun so they're happier in confinement. It's different for every animal. For the tiger we spray the log in his exhibit area with musk oil. You should see him when we do. He rubs his cheeks all over the log so lovingly. It's very sweet."

"So I'm supposed to help them be happy *in jail* . . . is that it?"

Just Carol smiles. "Something like that. Interested?"

I shrug. "I guess," I say warily, trying to act as if I don't much care either way.

"Good," she says, and she is smiling again. A big smile, like the sun is shining after a long rain.

This makes me angry. I feel as if I've been bought off. I start to tell her that I have changed my mind and I don't want to be some prison guard after all, but she has already floated off in a tinkle of bracelets and a sweep of her big colorful skirt. Then she is busy with the other kids and I forget about the mean things I want to tell her, because I'm wishing she would come again to talk to me.

6

ZOO TEENS

On Saturday, Just Carol picks me up at my house. Harrison is already in the car. I hope my mom doesn't see this. She said it was fine for me to go to the zoo, but I didn't exactly tell her Harrison would be there, too. I think my mom is still up in her room, so probably I'm all right. Elizabeth is outside, though. She's waiting for my mom to come down and take her to dance class. When she sees Harrison, she turns her head away and holds her nose. "L'air du salami," she says.

"Shut up!" I tell her. But actually, I'm happy to see Elizabeth. I was hoping she would see me get in a teacher's car. I have always thought teachers should drive station wagons or minivans or buses maybe. Not sports cars. But Just Carol's shiny new two-seater is clearly making a big impression on Elizabeth and I am suddenly glad this is what Just Carol drives.

Harrison and I sit together in the front seat with one safety belt around both of us. I'm wearing a jacket, although I'm too warm in it. I have to wear it because it's Pistachio's favorite jacket. The pockets are big, so they fit him better. I turn my hips toward the door and slip the seat belt up high so it doesn't squish him. I put some of my mom's perfume on, just in case Pistachio is smelling too doglike today. I even tried to put some on him, behind his ears, but it only made him sneeze.

I smile and wave at Elizabeth as if this is no big deal, we do this every Saturday. Elizabeth ignores me.

I know I should have left Pistachio home, but I couldn't bear to. When I picked him up at the vet's, I got little white pills for his heart. The vet said to give him one little white pill, three times a day. Just Carol said we would be at the zoo all day, so the only way I can give him his middle-of-the-day pill is if he comes with me.

I hate leaving him, anyway. I don't like to be left alone when I'm sick and neither does he. Though actually, he is much better. The pills are really helping him. He's almost his old self again. So, of course, this is when my mom remembers to check on him. "See? Didn't I tell you to wait a few days?" she asked as she watched him trot around the backyard. "Didn't I tell you he didn't need to go the vet?" This made me so mad, I came very close to telling her the truth and blowing everything. That's one problem with lying. Once in a while, it turns everything all around and the bad guys think they're the good guys.

"So why are you doing this, anyway?" I ask Just Carol.

"Doing what?" she asks me.

The inside of Just Carol's car is leather, the color of toast, and it's so clean, I wonder if it's new. If it is, she sure slapped a lot of bumper stickers on right away. Visualize Whirled Peas and Friends Don't Let Friends Go to Starbucks and a bunch of membership ones. Just Carol is a member of everything.

"Taking us to the zoo on your day off," I explain.

"I always go to the zoo on my day off. And I'm taking you because . . . Oh, I don't know. It's probably a bad idea." She looks over at me as if I will confirm this. I'm quiet, wondering what's going on. I'm not used to adults doing things they think are a bad idea or sharing a seat belt with Harrison in the front seat of a sports car driven by a teacher. I look over at Harrison to see what he's thinking. He looks very happy, the way he does when he greets his chicken after a long day away. Neither of us is used to getting special privileges. At school it's always girls like Joyce Ann Jensen or Alexandra Duncan who get the treats. At home it's Elizabeth or Kate who get the special things. But today, it's Harrison and me.

"Maybe it's because I'm fond of Harrison and you remind me of me," Just Carol blurts out suddenly, as if she's been thinking about it and this is what she's come up with.

"Me?"

"You."

"I'm not anything like you. I am not anything like anybody," I say.

"Always so suspicious." She shakes her head, but her earrings don't tinkle the way they usually do because she's wearing tiny posts. Her bracelets are gone, too, and so are her big rings and her jangly necklaces. She has jeans and a T-shirt on and her eyes look small and watery, not dark and dramatic the way she makes them up for school. She does not look like herself at all.

"Well, I'm not like you," I say.

"So you said."

"So what made you say I was?"

Just Carol looks into the rearview mirror to see if it is safe to change lanes. "When I was a kid, I never trusted anyone, either," she says.

"I trust Harrison," I say.

Just Carol smiles and pats Harrison's cargo pant leg. "That makes two of us," she says.

I wait for her to say more, but she doesn't, so I watch the hills go by the window. One after another full of brown grass. In Las Vegas everything was flat and in Orange County there was nothing but apartments with little strips of grass by the sidewalk, and the hills were all stuffed full of houses. Here there is more room.

I've never been to this zoo before. And I've never, ever been to any zoo as an almost zookeeper. I'm wondering if I will get to wear a uniform, when I see the big zebra zoo sign. Just Carol turns up a small winding road and parks her car under a eucalyptus tree.

We follow her through a gate marked Exit, past some flamingos with legs as skinny as hanger wire, and an empty chimp exhibit. We go down a road and behind a gate with a sign that says Do Not Enter to a row of low buildings next to a big stack of chain-link fence parts.

The people behind the Do Not Enter sign are all wearing khaki pants and khaki shirts and big black rubber boots. Just Carol seems to know everyone. She nods and says hello to almost all the khaki people and takes us inside a round stucco building, which has lockers on one side and big silver feed bins on the other. On top of the lockers are cases of corn and mixed vegetables, boxes of tennis balls and pillow sacks, infant swings, and stacks of empty milk cartons.

It smells funny—warm and animal, like a pet store—and there are strange whooping, screeching noises that everyone is ignoring. I ask Just Carol who is making those noises. She says it's the gibbons calling other gibbons, they do that all the time. Then she hands me and Harrison each a pair of big black boots. They are way too big for us, even with the extra socks she told us to bring. We wear them anyway.

Pistachio is wiggling in my pocket, as if he wants to get out. I don't think he likes the gibbons' whoops that build to an alarming pitch, like some kind of animal siren. Or maybe it's the strange smells that have him interested. I stick my hand in my jacket pocket and search for his belly, which I rub, hoping he won't groan.

"So this is them?" a khaki lady with very short black hair asks Just Carol.

"Ant, Harrison, this is Mary-Judy," Just Carol says. Mary-Judy is short for an adult—a lot shorter than I am. She has big solid legs like a rhino's, perfect white teeth, and a pink strawberry mark on her cheek. I wonder at the name Mary-Judy. It doesn't sound like two names that usually go together.

"You know," Mary-Judy says, eyeing Harrison and me suspiciously, "I don't normally take kid volunteers on my string."

"What about Zoo Teens?" I ask Just Carol.

"That's a Children's Zoo program," Mary-Judy says. "It's only because Carol here has volunteered for me for so long. She persuaded me that you two were really nice kids, extra conscientious, and good at following rules. That's the only reason I agreed to take you on."

Harrison and I look at Just Carol. No one has ever described us as extra conscientious and good at following rules. Just Carol is nodding her head, though her smile looks a little wobbly.

"Oh yes," I say. "We never do anything we aren't supposed to do."

"Never," Harrison agrees.

"Never," Mary-Judy repeats, staring at a hole in Harrison's pants where the end of his pocket is sticking through. "Look, let's get this straight, you listen to what I say and you do exactly what I tell you. I don't give second chances. Not when your safety, my safety, and the safety of my animals are involved." Mary-Judy gives me a mean look. I take my hand out of Pistachio's pocket. I feel guilty about having him here, then I realize Mary-Judy is looking after her animals, just like I'm looking after mine. Mary-Judy would do the same thing if she were me.

"In fact," Mary-Judy says, "I don't give first

chances. If you give me the slightest reason to boot you off my string, I will in a hot second, without thinking twice about it. Understand?"

I nod my head. Harrison is nodding his head over and over again, as if someone has turned on his nod button.

"They'll be fine, Mary-Judy," Just Carol says as her hand disappears in a big Tupperware tub filled with cardboard egg cartons and reappears with a handful of live worms. I shudder. I'm not squeamish, but I never expected there to be a big bin of worms sitting right on the desk like that.

Just Carol tosses the worms in a small silver bowl half filled with cut-up oranges and apples and bananas. One of the worms tries to crawl out, but Just Carol pushes him back. She is casual about this, as if she has done it one hundred times before.

"They better be," Mary-Judy says as she opens the handle of a large walk-in refrigerator and comes out with a bucket filled with dead rats. "All right, let's get a move on," she says. I try not to look at the dead rats. But I can't help it. I check to see if their eyes are open. No. Thank goodness for that.

Mary-Judy and Just Carol are walking together now and Harrison and I are behind. I put my hand in my pocket to pet Pistachio. He is still anxious, though it's better now that we are outside, walking behind the Do Not Enter sign and up into the main zoo.

Harrison is searching in his pockets as we walk. First the easy ones in front. Then the hard-to-reach cargo ones down his leg. This slows us down and we lag behind Just Carol and Mary-Judy. They stop and wait for us. Harrison is half hopping, half walking, trying to hurry and hunt at the same time. Mary-Judy gives Harrison a strange look.

"Why is it you guys call Carol *Just* Carol?" she asks when we are caught up.

"Because she's Just Carol, not Miss or Ms. or Mrs. Anything," I explain as Mary-Judy unlocks a big brass padlock and unwinds a thick metal chain from around a chain-link fence.

"Cute," Mary-Judy snorts, though I can't tell if she means this is cute or not cute. She turns over a plastic-covered sign attached to the gate with a paper clip. Now it says: Warning, Keeper in Area: Authorized Persons Only. Wow! This is pretty great. I've never been an authorized person before.

"Step in the bleach," Mary-Judy commands, pointing to a plastic basin half filled with liquid. "I lost a lion to leptospirosis, I'm not taking any chances." She glares at us as if she is sure we are germ carriers. And just as I slap my boots into the basin, Harrison presses something into my hand. It's a Milk-Bone. I can tell by the shape. Only Harrison would have this in his pocket. He doesn't even have a dog. It worries me, though, because if he's figured out Pistachio's in my pocket, then maybe Just Carol and Mary-Judy will, too. I look at Harrison. He smiles his goofy smile.

Mary-Judy opens another lock and unwinds a heavy chain from around the door of a low cement block building. "During the day, the lions are out in the exhibit," she says, "unless it's pouring down rain, then I take pity on 'em and let them in. But at night, they stay in here."

It's cool and dark in the night house, and it reeks of bad meat and urine and mildew. I can feel Pistachio smells it, too, because he's scrambling in my pocket, trying to get out.

Then I see the lions. They are in chain-link cages along the back wall. One male and three females. They are so big! Their backs are as tall as my chest, each paw is as large as my head, each of their heads is the size of half of me.

Pistachio is twisting and squirming, trying his best to get out. I ease the Milk-Bone into my pocket. It doesn't help. Pistachio is too excited to eat.

The lions are pacing back and forth in their cages, making strange noises, almost like dog barks. This surprises me, but I'm glad about it. If Pistachio makes a noise, everyone will think it's the lions.

A female lion jumps up on a low wooden bench in her cage and then down again. Her paws strike the cement with a velvet thump.

"Stay here," Mary-Judy barks as she walks down the row.

Don't worry, I think.

"Hi, Peggy," Mary-Judy says to one of the lionesses, who is standing on her hind legs, her front paws resting on the chain link. She is taller than Mary-Judy, yet she doesn't look scary. Her posture is friendly. She is rubbing her cheek on the chain link. She looks as if she wants to rub her face on Mary-Judy. She is saying hello to her, I realize, half expecting Peggy to open her mouth and give the top of Mary-Judy's head a big lick. Now, all of the lions seem like giant house cats and I want to pet them really bad.

Suddenly the male roars and lunges at the chain-link cage. My heart jumps in my chest. I hop back. He bellows deep and loud. The sound fills the small building, like a stereo turned unexpectedly loud. He throws his weight at the fence, determined to bring it down.

"All right, Junior, that's enough," Mary-Judy says. "For goodness' sakes! Why the dominance display? I'm just trying to see if you ate your supper last night." Mary-Judy walks in the empty chain-link cage next to the one where the male lion lives. She is even closer to him now. Is she nuts? Isn't she afraid? Mary-Judy is leaning over, looking for something.

"God, I need glasses," Mary-Judy says as the lion roars again and lunges at the fence, which bows with his weight. Mary-Judy is still leaning down. Why doesn't she get out of there?

But suddenly the male lion seems to lose interest. He turns and paces the distance of the cage. He sniffs the ground. He looks at us. He licks the fence—the tip of his big pink tongue curls through the chain-link diamond and he rolls his cheek against the mesh. He is easy now, content, sweet almost, as he swings his hind end toward us, lifts his tail high, and then I feel something wet. My hands fly to my face. Harrison pushes me. His elbow pokes my collarbone.

"Honest to God, Junior." Mary-Judy shakes her head.

It seems like the lion just sprayed us with pee, but

I can't quite believe this. The lion leaps on the wooden platform in his cage. He looks proud of himself.

"Yuck," Harrison says. "Chickens never do that."

"He's marking his territory," Just Carol says.

"We're his territory?" I ask.

"Apparently so," Just Carol answers.

Mary-Judy laughs in a friendly way. "Welcome to the zoo, ladies and gentlemen," she says. She shakes her short-haired head again. The way she does this, it seems as if there's something missing from her head. I wonder if she used to have long hair. "That's okay, guys. It's happened to all of us one time or another. It's my fault for not warning you. Someone here wearing perfume?" Mary-Judy looks at me.

I shrug. "Just a little," I say, edging myself away from Just Carol. Pistachio is wiggling like crazy. The smell is making him nuts. I hope he doesn't sneeze. I wonder if it will look suspicious if I walk out the door. I edge toward it.

Mary-Judy nods her head and puckers up her mouth. "That's why. Junior here likes perfume. He's particularly fond of the real musky ones. We always tell our keepers not to wear scents, because you never can tell what an animal will make of them. Especially one of our cats. You wouldn't believe some of the things perfume is made of—squashed beaver testicles, whale vomit . . . and who knows what those kinds of scents signify to a lion."

Mary-Judy is clearly enjoying herself now. She walks to the back wall, where there are pulleys marked with numbers. She grabs ahold of number 3 and hauls it down. The pulley makes a noise like rusty metal threading rusty metal and pulls open a door, which leads out of one of the lions' cages into the big exhibit area outside. The lion darts out, even before the door is all the way open. The way she moves, I know this is what she has been waiting for. Mary-Judy lets the pulley go back up, and the door comes down again, closing off the bright square of sunlight. The pulley door gives me the creeps. It reminds me of a guillotine I saw in a book at school.

Now Mary-Judy walks to pulley number 2 and does the same thing. When all the lions are out, she is all business again. "Carol, I think I have a couple of clean shirts hanging in my locker. Why don't you have Ant and Harrison put those on. I'm going to check the birds. I'll meet you at the African exhibit. We'll clean here after break." Mary-Judy picks up the bucket of rats and the bowl with the fruit and worms, then she waits for us to leave the night house first. When we are out in the bright sun, she wraps the heavy chain around the door and locks it with the kind of padlock Harrison uses on his bike.

7
KIGALI

Harrison and me didn't really get much pee on us, but we're not about to turn down the chance to put on khaki shirts that say Ziffman Park Zoo on them. These are the kind only the real keepers get to wear. Of course, I have to cover mine with Pistachio's jacket, which is the only part of me that actually got wet. I roll the sleeve up where it got a little pee on it and try not to get grossed out about it. I wonder what Your Highness Elizabeth would do if she got lion pee on her. This makes me laugh.

When Harrison comes out of the rest room, he looks almost like a real keeper. Harrison is kind of small, so the sleeves are way too long. I help him roll them up, then we crowd in front of the scratched-up old mirror attached to the inside of Mary-Judy's locker and admire ourselves.

Just Carol sticks her head in the locker room. "All right, you're both gorgeous. Now come on, you two. We've got a lot to do before lunch." I jump when I hear her voice, afraid for a second Pistachio is out of my pocket. But he isn't. He is curled in a little ball against my hip. I wish again I'd left him home.

When we get to the giraffe exhibit, there are pigeons everywhere—on the ground, in the mangers, under the wheelbarrows, and clustered in the doorways of the giraffe night houses. Everything is really tall here, like it was stretched in a fun-house mirror. The only regular-size part is the feed shack, which is lined with shiny silver trash cans and smells like hay and gingerbread.

The giraffes are already out in the exhibit area, and Mary-Judy is busy filling big black buckets with water and yelling at the pigeons. "Get out of here, you stupid birds." She squirts them with her hose and they scatter, making funny gobbling, cooing noises. When she sees us, she calls out, "You know, I thought maybe you and Harrison might feed Kigali. The bucket is ready. You show them, Carol."

Just Carol laughs through her nose. She shakes her head. "You two sure won her over. Getting to feed Kigali is a *huge* treat. Come on," she says, and leads us back around to the little feed shack. She opens the lid of a shiny new trash can and pulls out a blue bucket half filled with little green pellets. "You gotta hide everything here or the pigeons will eat it," she explains.

We follow her to a steep set of wooden steps that lead to a platform attached to the side of the exhibit area. Harrison gets his turn first. He climbs the steps with the awkward bucket banging his chin. When he gets to the top, three giraffes hurry toward the platform, their necks bobbing with each step. Up close their eyes look as if someone has applied thick black eyeliner to them, and their top lips hang over their bottom lips, like a bad case of buck lips. But it's their long necks I notice most—how elegant and graceful they are and how they move in directions my neck won't go. Squat-neck Elizabeth would be so jealous.

"Don't feed the others!" Carol warns Harrison. "Only Kigali. She's the old one with the blind eye. See her?" Carol calls. "The rest of them don't need extra food. Put the bucket behind you, Harrison, until they go away."

When Just Carol says this I wonder how we will know which giraffe is old. But then I see Kigali and I understand. Her bones poke out and the skin sags between them. Her coat is dull. One eye is a perfect white ball, as blank as the moon and all runny around it and stuck with dirt. She moves stiffly and her bones creak when she walks.

"Sometimes she's a little scared at first," Carol calls up to Harrison.

Kigali sniffs Harrison all over, almost like a dog. Her good eye seems to be inspecting him.

"She's checking him out," Carol whispers to me.

And then, all of a sudden, Kigali decides Harrison is okay and dips her head into the blue bucket. Now all I see are her horns, like big brown Q-tips sticking out. When she comes back up, she has a mouthful of tiny green pellets, which she chews in great circle motions.

"I think she likes me," Harrison calls down. He's smiling so wide, you can see his gums.

When it's my turn, I climb the steep ladder partway up. There's not really room for both of us on the platform up there.

"Hey, sweet Kigali, are you the nicest giraffe in the whole world? I think you are, Kigali. I think you are," Harrison whispers. Kigali's tongue is black, as if she's been eating licorice, but her spit is all slobbery and green.

"Is that good, sweetheart?" he asks.

I have heard Harrison sweet-talk his chicken this way when he doesn't know I'm around. He has forgotten it's my turn now. I put my hand in Pistachio's pocket and pet him. He's sleeping, I think. Apparently, nap time is nap time, zoo or no zoo.

Kigali and Harrison seem to see me at the same time. Kigali pulls her head out of the bucket, faces her good eye at me, and backs away. Harrison seems very sorry I am here. He doesn't let go of the bucket.

"Just let her come to you, Ant. Harrison, you can come down now. It's Ant's turn," Just Carol says.

Usually Harrison does anything Just Carol says. But not this time. Harrison doesn't move.

"He's got to stay up here, too. Kigali trusts him. She won't come over unless he's here. And besides, I'm afraid of her," I call down to Just Carol as I edge my way onto the platform with Harrison. It's squishy with both of us up here.

Harrison smiles at me. Just Carol snorts. All three of us know this isn't true.

I let Harrison hold the bucket and Kigali approaches again. Kigali gives me a once-over with her good eye, then ducks her head back in the bucket.

"Ant, think my dad will let me have a giraffe?" Harrison asks.

"If anyone would, it would be your dad," I say. I take his free hand. I can feel the callus on the side of his middle finger where he holds his pencil tight. I squeeze his hand, then I let go. My face feels hot, and I hope Just Carol didn't see. Harrison will understand I didn't mean anything by this, but no one else will.

8

THE LIONS

Harrison is still at the giraffe exhibit. Mary-Judy said we had to split in teams. We tried to get her to let us be a team together, but she said no way. She did say we could choose who would go where, though. Of course, I let Harrison stay with the giraffes and Just Carol and me head back to the lions' night house.

I stick my hand in my pocket. Tashi is quiet. He's probably on overload from all the smells. I pet his bristly fur with my finger and feel his hot breath on my hand. He is going to need to pee pretty soon, so I'm going to have to come up with a reason to sneak off by myself. I guess I'll say I have to go to the bathroom. They won't follow me in there, that's for sure. He seems peaceful right now, though, so I'll wait until he gets antsy again.

Just Carol has a dustpan in her hand. She hands it to me and pulls another one off a nail on the wall. "Scoop up the poop and the old meat, then put it in your bucket," she explains. "I'll take the front. You take the back. We'll meet in the middle." I nod and walk back to lions' cage number 5, trying to pretend I do this all the time. I look at the pulley that operates the metal door leading to the exhibit area. I know I'm safe so long as I don't pull it. Still, it feels spooky being caged in a cell that only a little while ago held a lion. I look at the metal door. There is a gap between the door and the floor. I see four lion legs walk by, close enough for me to touch. The hairs on the back of my neck stand up like little antennae.

From the inside, the cage looks like a cartoon prison cell. There is one long wooden bench, and that's it. The cage is just wide enough for a twin bed. I imagine the place all decorated with furniture and pictures. I wish I could fix it up, because it feels cold and empty the way it is. It makes me sorry for the lion who has to spend her night here.

In the corner there is a pile of poop, which looks like extra large dog poop, and at the other end, a scattering of old meat that smells like raw turned food. A bone the shape of a heart sits on the bench. I wonder what animal it has come from. The bone feels heavy in my dustpan the way a big rock would. I dump it in the bucket. The bucket smells so bad I have to hold my breath when I'm near it. After Just Carol and I get all the big pieces up, we turn on a black hose and spray the rest down a drain in the low center of the cement floor. The water sprays hard, like a fireman's hose. I like this part a lot.

I like working with Just Carol, too. She shows me what to do, but she isn't all teachery about it. She acts as if we are even-Steven here—like I am really a person, not just a kid. My mom is never like this. She is always the boss. Her job is to point out my mistakes, and as far as she is concerned, there are a million of them. I am wrong, even before I do anything. For one thing, I don't look right. She thinks I look like my aunt. And the way she feels about my aunt, this is like saying I look like a big blackhead. But she is wrong. I'm not ugly, I just don't fit in the same neat little box she and Your Highness and Kate do. I'm tall and dark. I have brown eyes and thick, thick hair that won't stay inside the hair baubles Kate and Your Highness wear. My nose has a bump on it, which is another thing that really bugs my mom. I think she would sand it off if she could. Your Highness and Kate both have small freckled noses "the size of rosebuds," my father says.

Sometimes my mom buys dresses that match for her and for us. They always have puffed sleeves and sashes and flocked flowers. I don't like them. I like my flannel shorts or my brown plaid pants or my orange jumper with all the zippers.

When I was little, my mother used to dress me in Your Highness's hand-me-downs. But now I'm taller than Your Highness, so my mom can't do that anymore. This is good, because I'd rather drink pee than wear Your Highness Elizabeth's clothes. My father says that Your Highness and I have normal "sibling rivalry" and it's because we are only one year apart that there is a problem. But this is not true. Even if we were ten years apart, I would still hate Your Highness Elizabeth. The only way we'd get along is if she died before I was born. Even then, I wouldn't want to wear her clothes.

Elizabeth never tries to be nice, but I think sometimes my supposed mother does. It's just that she can't. She sees a weed growing in the lawn and even if she's dressed in her best black dress, she can't stop herself from swooping down and snatching it out. And no matter what I do, I will always be a weed to her. I am all wrong. I set the table forks first. I keep my socks in my jeans drawer. I do the dishes sitting down. I eat in the bathtub. I read on the floor. I write notes on my hand or sometimes my leg. "This isn't the way people do things," she tells me, shaking her head, as if she is the keeper of the right ways to do everything.

It feels strange to squirt the lion's cage down with water and not be told I am doing it wrong. I wait to hear those words. My back is stiff to brace against them, but Just Carol seems only to make encouraging noises. "Hey, that's good, Ant. There, we got it. I think that's it, my dear!" she says. And suddenly I feel as if I might cry.

We are done cleaning the cages now. Carol opens the door of a refrigerator that sits against the side wall of the lions' night house. The refrigerator looks like ours at home, except there are no shelves inside. The only thing in it is an enormous piece of raw meat, which still looks like the cow it was. Just Carol saws off chunks with her knife. I feel queasy.

When she's done, there is a plate of neat red meat cubes. We take the meat and the cutting board outside so we can finish the rest of our work in the sunshine. We sit down on a bench in the shade of a big palm tree. I sit carefully so I don't bump Pistachio.

When I'm settled, Just Carol shows me how to cut a small hole in the meat and hide a white pill inside. "The lions take medicine for lepto . . . leptospirosis," she explains. "We put the pills inside the meat, then Mary-Judy feeds the meat squares to the lions on a long shish-kebab stick."

"Oh," I say, sticking one pill in a cube. I think I have it, then the pill pops out the other side and I have to dig another little hole for it. "So how come you work here every Saturday?" I ask as I pick the pill off the ground.

"Being around animals puts me in a good mood. It helps me keep things in perspective. It reminds me of when I was a kid and I wanted to be a vet."

I look at her frizzy yellow hair and her bright green eyes. She looks younger today than she normally does. She doesn't look like a teacher, either. If I didn't know better, I'd think she was an ordinary person.

"How come you didn't become one?"

"Too hard," she says.

"Really?" I'm amazed. Teachers never say things are too hard. Teachers make everything sound like it's supposed to be easy. Like writing a ten-page history report is more fun than a day at the beach.

"I'm not good at science," she says as she tips a pill in with the point of her knife.

"But you're a teacher," I say.

"I'm an art teacher. I did pretty well in English,

history, and art, of course. But not science. Chemistry—" She shakes her head. "Forget it."

I'm so surprised, I stop what I'm doing. She notices this and looks over at me. "Not everyone's as smart as you, you know," she says.

The smile comes to my lips before I can stop it. But as soon as I feel it there, I push it away. I don't want her to know how pleased I am. Still, I hope she will keep talking more about this. More about me and how smart I am.

"At least, that's what Sam Lewis says."

"Cave Man?"

Carol laughs a funny laugh, kind of a snort. "I guess I should feel lucky that I'm only 'Just' Carol and not something worse. Anyhow, Sam Lewis says you try to pass your work off as Harrison's. He says you even try to copy that weird handwriting Harrison has."

"Not anymore," I say as I pick up another chunk of meat.

"Yes, he said he talked to you about it and got you to stop."

I bite the pouch of skin under my lip. I want to tell her this isn't true. That he only thinks we've stopped. That we've outsmarted him. That we switch report cards now. But I know I shouldn't. She has two strikes against her. One, she's a teacher. And two, she told on me once already. I say nothing, the urge to brag practically choking me.

"We don't know why you did it, though."

I shrug. My mind clamps on the "we." Cave Man and Carol have talked about me? I like this idea.

"No really, Ant, why?"

"Harrison's father likes it when Harrison gets good grades," I say.

"Harrison's not stupid—why doesn't he do his own work?" she asks as she finishes her last cube.

I shrug again. "He'd rather draw."

She sighs and shakes her head. "Well, what about you? Aren't your parents, or whatever you call them, upset when you bring home bad grades?"

"They're used to it."

"Well, what do they think now that you got all those A's?" she asks, studying me as if the answer is somewhere on my face.

"They think I'm smart," I say, and I try to smile modestly while looking directly at her. Another good lying technique. Always hold a person's look. Never be the first to turn away.

"That's nice," she says as I feel something move in my pocket. Pistachio. I'd forgotten about him, but now he's getting restless.

We are done with our pill duty. This is my chance. "Look," I say, "I have to go to the bathroom."

"Okay." She picks up the plate of pill-stuffed beef chunks. "It's down by the front of the lion exhibit. It's all painted with zebra stripes. You can't miss it."

I go out the gate, step in the tub of bleach, then walk past the lion-viewing station to the zebra-painted bathroom. I'm smiling to myself. This Zoo Teen thing is really fun! But then the bottom drops out of my stomach when I remember the conversation I over-heard last Sunday. As soon as I get happy, then my dad quits his job and we move again.

I cut around behind the bathroom. Then, I look to see if it is safe to put Tashi down here. Nope. Too many kids by the lions' viewing area, so I cut through by the side of the exhibit. Two years is a long time, my brain tries to calm my stomach. And when we moved to Sarah's Road, he said it would be the last move. He said it would be forever. Besides, I asked him if we were moving and he said no.

I am near the lions now, but a safe distance from Just Carol and the public part of the zoo. This seems perfect, so I put Pistachio down on the dirt and right away he arches his back and sticks his nose and his tail in the air. He looks like a parade horse. I'm so happy to see him behaving like himself again, strutting around as if it's top secret business for him to smell ev-erything. I take off my jacket and toss it on a straw bale. I feel much cooler now. It really is too hot for a jacket, especially standing in the sun.

I sit down on the straw bale and wait for Pistachio to do his business. He is so busy smelling, he forgets to pee. "Go on, pee," I whisper. "We don't have all day, you know!" Once before, I left him too long in my pocket and he peed right there, a hot liquid running down my leg. I definitely don't want this to happen again. I look at the sun, wondering what time it is. Eleven? Eleven-thirty? This is close enough to the middle of the day, I think, so I take out Pistachio's tiny white heart pill and poke it down his throat, hold his mouth closed, and massage his neck the way the vet showed me how. Then I let him down. "Now, pee," I hiss at him, but he is so busy smelling the bale of straw that he pays no attention to me. He is very thorough about his smelling. One whiff won't do. He must smell every square inch. "Come on!" I say.

"Hey, Ant," Just Carol calls. Her voice seems close. Pistachio is down by the rocks now, sniffing his way to the chain-link fence. I wonder if I can get to him in time, when I hear Just Carol, even closer this time. "Ant?"

There's nothing I can do except hope she doesn't see Pistachio. "Yes," I say.

"Whatcha doin'?" she asks in an easy, friendly tone of voice.

"Oh, I was just looking at the lions," I say, nodding toward them and away from Pistachio. "They sure are lazy."

"A little nap, a sunbath, a sip of water . . . tough life, isn't it?" she says as Junior, the male lion, nuzzles one of the lionesses. Just Carol is absorbed in watching them, so I glance to see where Pistachio is again.

"You ready?" Just Carol asks. "Because it's lunchtime. Mary-Judy doesn't like it if we're late. She'll get worried the lions had an early dinner and come hauling up here in the zoo truck to find us." Just Carol smiles.

"Okay," I say. I will walk down a bit with her, then

tell her I forgot my jacket, which luckily I did take off. Then I'll run back and scoop up Pistachio. I glance at him. He is all the way over by the fence now.

"I know you brought your lunch . . . did you bring something to drink, too? I don't know about you, but I'm really thirsty," Just Carol says. She is walking fast. I am walking slow, hoping she will slow down, too. But she doesn't. She walks on ahead of me.

We are getting farther and farther away from Pistachio. My heart is jammed up in my throat and beating loud in my head. I'm sweating big drips. I steal a glance back and I see Pistachio's brown body near the lion chain link. The lions will eat him if he goes in there. This idea hits me hard, like I jammed my finger in the door. "Wait here!" I whisper. "I—I forgot my jacket." I am so scared, my throat has closed up. I can barely speak.

I run back, hoping she won't follow me, but I can't help it if she does, now. Pistachio is too near the fence. He is so small, he could go under. I head back to where I last saw him, but now I can't find him. I stop. I look around. Where is he? "Pistachio!" I call through my closed-up throat. Then I hear his high-pitched yip and I see the sudden excited motion of his small body out of the corner of my eye. I turn around. There he is. In with the lions. He's barking at them, his small tail straight in the air.

9

A HIPPOPOTAMUS OATH

At first, the lions ignore him. They are too busy sunning themselves to notice. Maybe they think Pistachio is a fake dog, or too little to care about one way or the other. I am almost to the fence now. "PISTACHIO! COME! COME!" I pound my leg with my hand.

Pistachio ignores me. He is jumping around, barking his head off, daring them to get him. Daring them to fight. Then, suddenly, one of the lionesses snaps to attention. Her whole body tenses. A streak of energy arches through her. She crouches and leaps, all in one smooth motion.

"PISTACHIO!" I scream, shoving my arm under the fence, trying to grab him. My fingers graze his bristly fur, but I get hold of nothing.

"What? What? Are you nuts?" Just Carol screams. I hear her rubber boots pounding toward me.

I am flat on the dirt with my arm as far under the fence as it will go. "PISTACHIO! PISTACHIO!" I call. The chain link is tearing my arm. I try to push closer to Pistachio. I touch his wiry fur again, trying to grab ahold, but he jumps out of my reach. Just Carol tugs at my other arm. "GET YOUR ARM OUT OF THERE!" she cries.

"LET GO!" I scream. The lion is there now. She has covered the ground in a flash. She lets out a terrifying roar and sails through the air. Pistachio is bark, bark, barking. I snap my eyes shut and yank my arm back without even thinking. I can't help myself. It's pure fear. Then I force myself to open my eyes. Oh, my God. She's eaten him. I hear a terrible noise as if someone is sobbing or moaning. It's coming from me. I want him back. I have to hold him again. I will do anything for this, and then I feel a scratching at my boot. I look down and there he is. Panting hard, wagging his tail a million miles an hour, looking eagerly at me as if he has just had a lot of fun.

"Holy Jesus!" Just Carol says.

I pick up Pistachio and hold him tight against me. I am never going to let him go again. I smell his dog smell, like leaves burning. He licks my finger with his small, wet, raspy tongue. The lioness is still watching him. She is pacing on the other side of the fence. Back and forth. Back and forth. I shudder. My whole body feels stiff, as if I've taken a hard fall. And my arm is bleeding a little where I scratched it on the chain link.

"What the hell were you doing?" Just Carol asks.

I don't say anything. I don't feel able to explain right now. I don't think my mouth will work. All I know is that Pistachio is here with me. I stroke his fur. He curls his body against mine and licks my hand all over as if it's dirty and he needs to make it clean. He seems proud of himself. I would hate him for this if I weren't so glad to have him safe. I'm shaking, I'm so grateful he is all right.

Just Carol is watching me. She is very quiet.

I get my coat, put it on, and pour Pistachio back in the pocket.

"So," she says. She's not moving. Not blinking. She is so still, I wonder if she is even breathing, but then I see her eyes are jumping mad. "He's been there all morning," she declares in a hard little voice.

She's walking now, and my legs are moving, too. We go around to the front and step in the bleach tub and walk down to the main zoo, through the gate that says Danger: Do Not Enter.

Just Carol doesn't say anything else. I steal a glance at her, wondering what will happen now. Her face is blank, it's only her teeth that give her away. They grind as we walk.

We are approaching the big feed room and the locker room. Harrison is sitting with Mary-Judy and three keepers at a picnic table just outside the door of the kitchen.

A khaki man is walking behind us. "Hey, what was all that commotion over by the lions?" he asks.

"What commotion?" Mary-Judy's hand freezes, holding the waxed paper from her sandwich.

"I don't know . . . sounded like maybe a keeper was in there." The man laughed.

"Yeah," said Just Carol. "It was Peggy. She climbed a tree after a squirrel. It was something." Just Carol smiles.

"Oh, is that all." Mary-Judy relaxes. "Did she get it?"

"Nope. Got to a high skinny branch where Peggy couldn't get her."

"Treed her, huh? Well, it's only a matter of time, then. That Peggy, she's good. I've seen her climb halfway up the chain link to get a squirrel. Scared me to death. I had maintenance double string the top of the whole exhibit after that."

"Well, so long as it's not you up there in that tree, Mary-Judy." The man laughs.

"If it is, you'll be the first to hear about it, Joe." Mary-Judy takes a banana out of her lunch bag.

"If we lose you, I have dibs on your radio," a tall, skinny khaki lady says. She takes a long drag from her cigarette.

"Honey, if I'm gone, you can have everything. Even my underwear," Mary-Judy says.

"Harrison." Just Carol beckons with her finger. Harrison jumps up and comes over to us.

"Wash your hands. Change out of your boots. We're going home," she whispers in a mean voice, like how she talks to kids she doesn't like.

"Why?" Harrison asks.

"Talk to your buddy here. She'll tell you." Just Carol nods at me.

Harrison's face scrunches all up.

"Hey, Carol, what's going on?" Mary-Judy asks.

"I'm sorry, Mary-Judy, but I think Ant's ready to go. A whole day is a little much first time out. I'm going to run the two of them home, then I'll be back," Just Carol says, as smooth as can be.

"So, you're stealing my helpers, are you. Just when I get them all trained."

"I'm sorry, Mary-Judy," Just Carol says.

"Tired you out, huh?" Mary-Judy says to me.

I nod. I am tired, I realize through the dull thudding of my head. But I'm also feeling guilty. Why does Harrison have to go home, too? This isn't fair.

We walk up out of the Do Not Enter area. I hear the sound of Harrison's sneakers and Just Carol's rubber boots slapping the ground when she walks. I smell the big eucalyptus trees and step on the acorns. The gibbons are quiet now, but the macaws are making a terrible fuss. It sounds as if they are arguing over something. A woman is pushing her child in one of the zoo's rental strollers. It rattles like an old grocery cart.

Just Carol doesn't say a word. Harrison is looking over at me through his straggly hair. He wants to know what happened, but I feel too lousy to explain.

It's a long way to the car with Just Carol and her silence and Harrison and his disappointed face, but we finally make it. Just Carol fishes the keys out of her pocket and unlocks the shiny doors. I am buckling the seat belt around Harrison and me when she lets me have it. "So why in God's name did you hide that dog in your pocket all morning? What is the purpose of a stunt like that? Did you plan to feed your dog to the lions or was that his idea?"

I take Pistachio out of my pocket and put him on my lap. Harrison sucks air in. "Is he okay?" he asks, running his hand along Tashi's head and down his back. He touches Tashi carefully, as if he is formed out of sand.

"Are you crazy? I'd never hurt Pistachio. Never. He just thinks he's a lot bigger than he is, is all. He's just really brave."

"Am *I* crazy?" Just Carol asks. "I'm not the one that stuck my arm in the lions' exhibit."

Harrison is scratching behind Pistachio's small triangle ears.

"Not only that," she begins, counting my sins with her fingers. "You put your own dog's life in danger. Not to mention sacrificing me. I actually care about being able to volunteer here, and I stuck my neck out so you could come. And . . ." Now she's on finger number four. "You could have gotten Mary-Judy in a whole bunch of trouble, because she's the one responsible for us, but that doesn't matter to you, either. Not to mention spoiling the chance for Harrison here. Did you think of that?" This is finger number five: Just Carol's thumb.

I look over at Harrison. His shoulders are hunched. He looks as if he wishes he could disappear. I don't think he's mad at me. He just hates fighting, especially between me and Just Carol. He likes us both too much.

"I had to bring Pistachio. I had to," I say.

"You had to? Why is that?"

"He has a heart problem. He has to have his pill. The vet said I have to give him pills three times a day. She said I couldn't miss one. You said we were going to be here all day. How else could I give him his middle-of-the-day pill?"

"Do you know how ridiculous that sounds?"

"It's true."

She groans and shakes her head. "Surely your mother or one of your sisters could have given him his pill."

"They don't know I went to the vet."

Just Carol grabs hold of the steering wheel with both hands, then turns to me. "Tell me, are you ever honest about anything? It seems as if everything you say is some kind of big secret or an out-and-out lie. What is the point?"

I say nothing. This is one of those questions that gets you in even more trouble if you try to answer it.

Just Carol turns the car on. We drive out of the zoo and onto the main road. I look out the window at the brown grass-covered hills again, but now I hate them. I wish they were all coated with houses and cement just like everywhere else I've lived.

Just Carol is ignoring me. I am angry. I don't make up lies for no reason. I just move the truth around a little when it gets in my way. What's the big deal about that? My mouth forms the words, but no noise comes out. I'm feeling so shaky from having come so close to losing Pistachio that everything feels all twisted around inside me. And I feel rotten about Harrison. I look over at him. He has combed all of Pistachio's hair with his hand.

Just Carol is driving fast. We're past all the brown

hills now and rapidly approaching the cutoff to Sarah's Road. We pass Fred's All-Natural Incense, the gas station with the big sign that says Smog Certificates, and the used-clothing store. For once I wish there was more traffic. Just Carol needs time to cool down. I want her to say something, but apparently she is done talking.

"Well, there *was* a reason," I say when we pass Albertson's Market, which is right next door to Marion Margo School of Ballet, where Elizabeth and Kate go. I look to see if Mrs. MacPherson's car is there. It isn't.

"A reason? A reason for what?"

"For why I couldn't tell my mom to give Pistachio a pill."

She sighs. "And what was that?"

"If she found out, she'd kill me. She thinks vets are too expensive. She says it's like pouring money down the drain."

"So you took him yourself."

"Yep." We pass the antiques store with the sign that says Back in 5 Minutes. As long as we've lived here, the sign has said this. My father says it's the longest five minutes in recorded history.

"How did you get there?"

"I walked."

"How did you pay for it?"

This question takes me by surprise. That's the trouble with the truth. One true thing leads to another and then pretty soon you've told everything. "I didn't. They were going to bill me and I didn't write down my address exactly right."

"You know that's against the law. It's like stealing from the vet."

"It's not about money. Vets care. They take a Hippopotamus oath when they become a vet, which says they will do their best to look after animals who need them."

"Hippocratic oath," she says. "So you brought your dog today—what's his name?"

"Pistachio."

"Pistachio, so you could give him his heart pill?"

"Yes."

We are at my house now. The front yard was all weeds when we moved here, but my mother has been working hard to make it nice. Mr. MacPherson says not to bother, it's a renter. But my mom can't stand to have things a mess. I open the car door, but I don't get out. "So what about next Saturday?"

"I don't think so," Just Carol says.

"Oh, come on, I was just taking care of my dog."

Just Carol looks out the window. Her eyes have a faraway look. "You know, you live in your own little world with your own twisted logic. But the trouble is, you never take anyone else into account. Not the vet. Not me. Not Mary-Judy. Not even your dog . . . Peanut or whatever his name is. He almost got eaten alive today."

"But he didn't. I saved him," I say.

"You didn't save him, you were just lucky. Really lucky. You could have lost your arm and your dog." She blows air out of her mouth. "Which is why it's not safe to take you to the zoo."

She is right about this. Pistachio could have been killed. I hold him tight against me to fend off this thought. "So why'd you cover for me with Mary-Judy, then?" I ask as I get out of the car.

"I didn't cover for you. I covered for me," she says as she flips the master lock switch and the little button goes down. "And Harrison."

"Bye, Harrison," I say, but Just Carol rolls up the passenger side window, so he doesn't hear me. I am sealed out.

After they're gone, I cradle Pistachio against my cheek. "I'm sorry," I say. He licks my eyebrow with his raspy tongue. He is never mad. Not ever. Dogs are better than people. They are.

10
DINNER AT THE MACPHERSONS'

My dad is home for Saturday and half of Sunday, then he has to go back to Atlanta. We won't do our usual celebration meal, though, because he's only been gone for a week. Still, my mom prepares a special dinner. She makes some kind of meat dish that looks way too orange. It's almost Day-Glo, the color of those vests the highway repairmen wear. I don't think food is supposed to be that color. I don't think Kate does, either. She has already managed to get my mom to give her extra rice and only a tiny speck of orange gunk all by itself.

I'm in the kitchen. Dad, Elizabeth, and Kate are at the table waiting. "Mom, do you think you could put the orange stuff on the side, please?" I ask as sweetly as I know how.

"The orange stuff?"

"The beef whatever you call it?" I better not make her mad or she'll ruin my nice white rice by slopping that stuff on it.

"Beef à l'orange," she says.

"It looks lovely, Mom." I smile sweetly. "But could you put it on the side . . . please?"

My mother glares at me. We both know I'm only being nice so she'll do this. But she's angry. I'm not sure why. Maybe it's because of what happened in Mr. Borgdorf's office the Tuesday before last. Or maybe it's something else. She is always mad at me about something. I am always a stone in her shoe.

My mother puts the orange gunk on the side.

"Thank you," I say, carrying my plate to the table.

"Daddy?" Elizabeth says.

"Yes, sweetheart."

"Did you get to play golf today?"

"No, honey, I had meetings all day." He smiles at her as if this is the nicest question anyone has ever asked him. Doesn't he know she's buttering him up?

"Daddy?" Kate asks. "Did you get to play golf *yesterday*?"

My dad smiles at Kate. "No, sweetie. I had to work then, too. But hopefully soon, I won't have to work so much."

"Why?" Elizabeth asks, her neck stiff, her eyes wary.

"I'm just getting my priorities straight. That's all." My dad puts his napkin in his lap.

"What does that mean?" Elizabeth asks. I am wondering the same thing.

"Daddy, do you know what? In ballet class I got to do a pirouette," Kate says.

My father shakes salt on his beef. "When you do

things I can't pronounce, I know that's something," my father says.

My mother laughs.

"And what about you, Little Brown Acorn?" My father takes a slice of bread and butters it. His cell phone rings. He pulls it out of his shirt pocket and pops it open. "Don MacPherson." He listens for a full minute. It's quiet, except for the sound of my mom sawing her meat. "Yes, Dave. You know, I just sat down to dinner with my family. Could I call you back? . . . Uh-huh. Look, Dave . . . I know for a fact they made their numbers in September. Maybe they weren't leading the pack, but . . . All right. I don't have them in front of me now. Could I call you back after dinner?

"I'm sorry, honey," my father says. He flips his cell phone closed and slips it into his pocket. His mouth is smiling, but his face is frowning.

Sometimes I wish I worked with my dad. I have been to his office, but it's just desks and computers and phones and stuff. I don't get what's so urgent about it. It seems pretty boring to me.

"What did Dave want?" my mother asks.

"Forget Dave. I'm not going to ruin my dinner by talking about Dave. Here I am with my wife, who just happens to be the most beautiful woman in the world. You bet. You bet she is . . . and my daughters, who are beautiful and graceful and intelligent." He smiles at us. I like how he says this. It feels as if he loves us, all three the same. "My daughters are going to be famous ballerinas. Oh yes, yes, they are!"

"What about Antonia? Antonia isn't going to be a famous ballerina," Kate says.

"What?" My father seems startled.

"Antonia," Kate says, "she's not going to be a famous ballerina."

Elizabeth snorts.

"Elizabeth!" my mother says.

"Antonia, yes, well, she's a special case, isn't she." He nods his head and sucks his lips in as if he's considering this. "Antonia is going to be . . . she's going to be . . ." He raises his wineglass high. It glistens in a spike of light. He looks at me. He winks. "She's going to be . . ."

It feels like the pointy end of a pencil digging in my chest. The longer the pause, the deeper the point goes. I look down at the plastic place mat, which is curling up at the corner. "Antonia is going to be . . ." He thrusts his glass in the air again, as if the momentum will help him get through this.

"A juvenile delinquent," Elizabeth offers.

My father's head drops back and he laughs loud and hard. Not because he thinks this is funny, but because Elizabeth saved him and now he's covering for himself.

My lungs feel flat, as if no matter how hard I breathe I won't be able to get air in them. He didn't even know enough about me to guess. He didn't know enough to lie.

He takes a bite of his orange meat. "This is wonderful, honey," he says.

"I'm going to be a zookeeper," I say. "In fact, I already am one."

"Ah yes, well, the zoo is a good place for you, Antonia," my mother says.

I look her full in the face.

"I just mean because you like animals." My mother smiles her fake sweet smile. My mother likes to sneak mean things into the conversation, then pretend she didn't mean them.

"As a matter of fact, I already have a job at the zoo," I say.

"Do not," Kate says.

"Do, too," I say. "I'm a zookeeper. A real one. I get to go where nobody except real zookeepers go. Like inside lions' cages and stuff." I don't tell the part about the lion marking his territory, because my mom will think this is gross and then she might not let me go again. Not that I'm going to be able to, anyway, given how mad Just Carol is. "Today I got to feed a giraffe," I say. "She licked my hand."

"That is *so* disgusting!" Elizabeth says.

"Sure you did," Kate says. She rolls her eyes and flickers her eyelids. "And I've got ten million dollars in my bank account."

"Tell them, Mom. Tell them I went to the zoo! I wore rubber boots and a real shirt and everything."

"Well, I *hope* you wore a shirt," Elizabeth says.

Mr. MacPherson laughs his short, loud laugh.

"No, a *zookeeper* shirt."

"Well, I hope you get to keep your shirt," Kate says.

She looks at my dad and mom. She is so proud she's come up with this. "Keep your keeper . . . get it?"

Mr. and Mrs. MacPherson both laugh. His short and loud. Hers more of a giggle.

I hate that they're doing this. I feel like screaming STOP as loud as I can. "Do you want to see? Because I can show you." I push my chair back from the table. No one pays attention. They are too busy with their jokes.

I run upstairs to my room and come back with Mary-Judy's shirt. It says Ziffman Park Zoo on a badge on the side. There's no doubt this is real.

"See," I say, breathing hard from the run up and down the stairs. I hold the shirt up and wiggle it at them. "They only give these shirts to real keepers, *who get paid.*" I'm not sure why I add this, but somehow I need to.

"I thought it was a field trip. You're getting paid?" my mother asks.

"Yes, I am," I say. I look her straight in the eye.

"How much?" my father asks. Now I have his interest. He likes things that make money.

How much would seem believable, I wonder. Ten dollars? Too much. Two dollars? Not impressive enough. "Five dollars an hour," I say.

"Really?" He waves a fork full of Day-Glo orange meat.

"You are not getting paid," Kate says. "I know how much you have."

"I haven't gotten paid *yet*, I just started today," I say.

"I don't believe you," my mother says, dabbing the corner of her mouth with her napkin.

"What else is new?" I say.

"Oh, look, don't make this my problem."

I shrug, but say nothing. In an argument, it's always better when the other person is upset and you stay calm, as if you can't understand why they're so aggravated.

"Well, you know, honey," my father says. "They might have a reason to be paying those kids. It's cheap labor. With kids, you don't have to pay benefits and you don't have to pay a living wage, either. Just enough. Like an allowance, really."

"I doubt it, Don. There are laws against child labor, you know . . . ," my mother says.

"Laws, shmaws. Wherever there's a law, there's a loophole. That's Murphy's Law of government, Evelyn," my father says.

My mother laughs. She raises her hands as if she's giving up. "Fine, when you get your first paycheck, I'd like to see it, Antonia," she says.

Dear Real Mom,

I don't want to be a zookeeper when I grow up. And I don't get paid to work at the zoo, either. I know you know that. But this is okay because it's only a little green lie. Little green lies are the kind you have to tell to keep safe. It's like when chameleons change colors to camouflage themselves so predators don't eat them. No one thinks that's a lie. Everyone thinks that's perfectly fine, because otherwise how would they survive.

I know you understand. And I know someone like Just Carol never will. She thinks I should say that I'm really doing well in school, especially in math. Someone like Just Carol thinks it's so easy to say this. She thinks it makes all the sense in the world to be honest this way. But someone like Just Carol doesn't understand you can't go around telling the truth all the time. You have to be careful with it. You can't waste the truth on people who won't understand.

Love,
Ant and Pistachio

11
THE POSTCARD

It's Wednesday evening and I'm on the phone talking to Harrison.

"You have to ask your mom if you can come over. You have to. We've got stuff to do," Harrison says.

Elizabeth picks up the downstairs extension. "Come on, *you kids,*" she says. "Get off! I've got an important call to make."

"I still don't see what we need to do at your house," I say, ignoring Elizabeth. I am used to her butting in this way.

"We got to plan our apology," Harrison explains.

"What's there to plan? I just say I'm sorry," I say.

"Sorry? Sorry for what?" Elizabeth asks.

I put my hand over the receiver and scream down at Elizabeth, "GET OFF! IT'S NOT YOUR TURN!"

"No, Antonia! I need to make an important call *right now,*" Elizabeth says into the phone.

"Hold on," I tell Harrison. I put the receiver down and run downstairs.

"GET OFF!" I scream at Elizabeth.

"You can talk to Harrison any old time. I have to call someone *important*. It's like 911," Elizabeth says.

"911?"

"*Like* 911, I said," Elizabeth says.

"What's the emergency?"

"None of your business."

"Fine, you wait, then," I tell her.

"You know, Antonia, I heard Pistachio just a minute ago. He was coughing. It didn't sound good. If I were you, I'd go check on him. Maybe he . . . you know." She sticks her tongue out and hangs her head, like she is cartoon dead.

"You've been in the kitchen. You couldn't have heard anything."

"Before I was downstairs I was upstairs," Elizabeth says.

"Oh, right," I say. I know this is another ploy and I hate Elizabeth for it. But it gets me just the same. Once I start worrying about Pistachio, I can't stay on the phone. I don't know why we don't get a cordless phone, then I could talk in my own room with Pistachio curled up next to me. Everyone in the world has a cordless phone except us.

I grab the receiver from Elizabeth. "I'll call you back, Harrison," I say.

My mother comes in the kitchen just as I'm running out to check on Pistachio.

"What's all this racket about?" my mother asks.

"Antonia is being a phone hog. Like always," Elizabeth says.

"Hang up the phone up there, Antonia!" my mother

yells after me. "And then come down here, I want to talk to you!" I'm at the top of the stairs now. Elizabeth is right behind me.

I look in on Pistachio. He jumps up and wags his little tail when he sees me and practically leaps into my arms. I take him back into the hall. Of course, Elizabeth has the phone pulled inside her room now. The cord is stretched tight. It isn't long enough to get to my room, only her room. But she can't get the door shut over the curly part, so I can still hear. I stop to find out who she is calling that is *like 911.*

"I'd like to speak with Don MacPherson, please," she says in her most sophisticated voice.

Dad? She's calling DAD. Oh, this will be good. I lean into the door and listen as hard as I can.

"He isn't. I see. And when do you expect him back?"

I marvel at the way she says this. Everything about it sounds so grown-up. Even the tone is smooth, as if she's said this a million times before.

"Okay. Good. No, no message. Thank you," Elizabeth says. Her voice sounds relieved.

How weird. I'm about to go in and ask her what in the heck she's doing calling Dad, when my mom calls up the stairs. "Antonia, didn't I ask you to come down?"

I shrug. "I'm sorry, I didn't hear you." I walk downstairs, holding Pistachio against my belly.

"You know, Antonia, you really must learn to share," my mother says.

I think about telling her the truth, but it won't do

any good. I follow her into the kitchen, where she sits on a stool. There's a catalog in front of her and a stack of mail on the counter. Uh-oh. What's this about? Is there a bill from the vet here? Did they track me down from Pistachio's license number? No, I decide. If there was a bill, my mother would be so angry, she would have stormed upstairs to get me. This is something different.

I pull out a white wooden chair and plunk myself down. My mother gives me the evil eye and shakes her head. "Antonia," she says, "must you sit down as if your legs have been pulled out from under you?"

I shrug, hoping this isn't going to be one of her you-must-be-more-ladylike lectures. I hate all that ladylike stuff. I'm not a tomboy. I just don't see why being a girl should mean I have to follow a bunch of stupid rules about how I sit, who opens the door, and how often I do the dishes.

"I don't understand you," my mother says. This is the way she often starts her talks with me. She's not as angry as usual, though. And she has paused after saying this, as if she actually wants a response this time. I look around the kitchen. Everything is neat. It's always this way. Even when my mother is cooking a big meal, she still manages to keep the place clean. Not Mr. Emerson. When Mr. Emerson cooks, his kitchen looks as if somebody has turned the room upside down and everything has spilled out.

"I got this notice from your school a few days ago." She's holding a small yellow postcard in her hand. "It says because you are doing so well in math, you've been invited to attend the District 2 Math-a-thon."

I smile when I see this. I can't help myself. We had a math test a couple of weeks ago and the six highest scorers got picked for this. I can't believe one of them is me. I am so pleased it is practically busting out of me.

"I was sure they'd made a mistake, because the last report card I got said you got a D in math, so I called up your teacher, Mr. Lewis, and he told me he gave you an A in math." My mother puts the card down and takes a sip of coffee. Then she looks at me, as if I am a puzzle and she is trying to figure me out.

I look down at the tabletop. I trace the lines with my finger. I am busy marveling at myself. Apparently I scored higher than practically everyone else!

"Actually," my mother says, "Mr. Lewis said if there was anything higher than an A you would have gotten that. He said he thought you were testing at a tenth- or eleventh-grade level in math."

She waits a minute for this to sink in. She is watching me and I am watching the sugar canister. I trace the letters S-U-G-A-R with my eyes.

"You can imagine how embarrassing this was," she starts in again. Her brown eyes are watching me. "How very stupid it made me look that here I think my child is flunking when she's at the top of her class. But then I've come to expect these little surprises from you. And once I got over feeling angry, I began to wonder why on God's green earth you would do this. Why you'd want me to think you were doing poorly when you were really doing well. You know, Antonia, I have no idea why you do these things. I really don't understand the first thing about you."

I wonder if I should nod my head. She is right, but will it make her angry if I agree with her? Usually the more I say, the longer my mother grounds me for.

"Why did you do this?" she asks.

I shrug, like what's the big deal.

She takes a deep breath and seems to try to relax. "Why do you lie when it would be easier to tell the truth?"

"Easier for who?"

My mother groans and shakes her head. She puts her hand on her forehead as if she has a headache. "Easier for everyone. If you told the truth . . . ," my mother starts. "Oh, Antonia, I am so tired of having these discussions with you. . . ."

I shrug again. "Whatever," I say. I don't look at her when I say this, though. I'm suddenly so disappointed, I can't bear to look her in the eye. There is nothing I can do to please my mother. Nothing.

Later, when she's gone, I go down and get the postcard. I want it for my real parents' book. This is the first time I've been asked to be in a Math-a-thon. My real parents will be pretty excited about this. They'll realize that only six students in my whole grade got invited. They'll figure this out right away!

12
ELIZaBETH'S DRESS REHEaRSaL

When I wake up Sunday morning, I go downstairs to take Pistachio out.

My mom is in her turquoise terry cloth bathrobe. She is getting a can of OJ concentrate out of the freezer. She looks fuzzy, like she's not quite awake. When my dad is home he bounces out of bed, ready to do battle. My mother must ease herself into the day, the way a very old lady pulls herself to a standing position.

Usually, I try not to talk to her about important stuff until later in the day, but this can't wait. Last night Harrison called to say I had to come over to his house first thing this morning so we can plan how to convince Just Carol to take us back to the zoo. He said we had to act fast, because Kigali needed him and she can't wait. "What if she decides she won't eat for anyone else?" he asked. I told him he should go to the zoo without me. But he said: "Forget it, Ant. Just forget it."

"Good morning, Mom," I say.

She squints at me, as if anyone who says this is suspect. "Antonia?" she asks. She dumps the concentrate out of the can and turns on the tap. Her actions are jerky and automatic, as if she is being operated by a remote control.

"I need to go to Harrison's house," I explain. She is stirring with a long wooden spoon.

"Antonia?" she interrupts me. "Not so loud, okay?"

"Okay," I whisper. "I need to go over to Harrison's house on account of it's important for school."

She squints again. Mrs. MacPherson hasn't put her contacts in yet and I don't think she sees very well without them. She pats at her bathrobe pocket to see if her glasses are in there. They are. She puts them on.

"For school?" She looks at me funny, like she doesn't believe me.

"Kind of only because a teacher is mad at us and we have to figure out how to get her un-mad." I hadn't planned on telling her the truth here. I surprise myself sometimes.

"Oh," she says. She nods like she believes me. People being mad at me makes a lot of sense to her.

"Fine," she says.

"Fine? Aren't you going to ask why?"

"Don't press your luck, Antonia, I said fine. And no, I don't want to know why you're in trouble again. When you come home, take your shoes off outside and go straight into the bathroom and take a shower. I won't have my house smelling like chickens and God knows what else. And be careful what you eat there. In fact, maybe you shouldn't eat anything at all. And wash your hands . . ."

But I don't hear the rest because I'm running upstairs to call Harrison. "Harrison?" I say when I hear his voice on the phone. "She said I could."

"YES!" Harrison yells so loud, I have to pull the receiver away from my ear.

"I'll be over in an hour," I say when he calms down.

"No. Now. I'll get my dad to pick you up."

Apparently, Harrison has a plan. This is the only time he gets bossy. I get Pistachio and put him in his favorite coat pocket. Not to hide this time, just because he likes it there.

"I thought you were going to Harrison's," my mother says when I go back downstairs.

"I am. His dad's going to pick me up."

Kate comes in the kitchen. She's carrying her notebook. She sees I have my jacket on and Pistachio is in my pocket. "Where are you going?" she asks. Her pencil is poised waiting to record what I say.

"To Harrison's house," I say.

"Does Mom know?" she asks.

"Yes, Mom knows," Mrs. MacPherson says.

Kate nods. Her curls flop around her face. It doesn't look as if she's brushed her hair yet this morning.

"Oh, and by the way, what time is your Math-a-thon week after next?" my mom asks. "I wrote down the twenty-eighth, but I didn't write down the time. I thought I had that postcard here, but it seems to have disappeared. Did you see it, Antonia?"

I tear at my thumbnail. Not saying anything isn't lying, it's just not saying anything.

"Good morning." Your Highness pushes through the kitchen door. She's wearing pink tights and a pink sweater and her hair is neatly combed in a ballerina bun. Elizabeth is great at making appearances. When she walks into a room, it always seems as if she's expecting to be handed a bouquet of flowers.

"Good morning," my mother says. "The reason I am asking is Elizabeth has a dress rehearsal on the twenty-eighth, too."

I look down at the chipped Formica counter. My finger traces the uneven shape that has chipped off, revealing the wood underneath. I breathe short, like my lungs are rolled up inside me.

"Antonia?" my mother asks.

"It's ten o'clock," I say, shoving my finger against the grain of the wood, hoping for a splinter.

"That's when my dress rehearsal is, Mom, and you have to go to that! You *promised* you would. Angela Beaumont's mom is going. Angela Beaumont's mom goes to everything!" Elizabeth says to my mom.

"Well, maybe I could go for part," my mother suggests. "Or maybe if Dad's home he can go to one and I can go to the other."

"*Both* of Angela Beaumont's parents go for the *entire time*," Elizabeth says.

My mom looks at Elizabeth. She looks at me. She bites her lip. "Well, I did commit to that first, Antonia," my mother says. "I'm supposed to bring the lemonade."

The old pain rises in my chest. I try to shove it back down. So what if she would rather see Elizabeth's four hundredth dress rehearsal than my first Math-a-thon?

So what? She isn't my real mother, anyway. It doesn't matter. "Don't worry. You're not invited to the Math-a-thon, Mom," I say, my voice calm, even, unemotional.

Frown lines cut across my mom's forehead. "But I thought that postcard said . . ."

I shake my head. "They decided there isn't enough room for the parents. They were going to hold it in the gym, but then they couldn't get the gym. And there isn't enough space in the library for a big audience. But they didn't know this when the postcard went out. They told us to tell our parents." I make my face all sincere and I look straight into my mom's eyes. *Please don't believe me*, a voice deep inside me begs. *Please come. I want you to come.* But I stuff the voice down.

"Oh." She shrugs. "Well, I guess that solves my problem, doesn't it?" Her face lights up. She smiles her wide-toothed smile.

I feel as if somebody has taken pliers to my insides.

The fake-music doorbell chimes. It sounds like somebody died.

"Who is that?" my mother asks.

Kate races to the door and presses her nose against the Coke-bottle-glass window that runs alongside the door. "It's Harrison's dad," she reports.

"Well, I guess you're going, then," my mother says to me. "But I look like a train wreck, so don't you dare ask him in."

"Okay," I say, and I'm out the door, whisking Mr. Emerson back down the front path. I want out of there. I don't want to give my mom the chance to change her mind. It was only last month she said I was not allowed to set foot in the Emersons' house "until hell freezes over," and now here I am planning to spend the day there with her complete permission. I should be happy about this, but I'm not.

13
THE EMERSONS

The Emersons have a funny house. On the outside it looks like a farmhouse and a big old barn, only there isn't any cropland. Just a yard with a palm tree. On the inside, it's filled with carpet pieces from Harrison's Aunt Sue's carpet store. There isn't much in the way of furniture, though, unless you count the beanbag chairs. They are everywhere. At the Emersons they either don't have something or they have it in quantity, like there's never any scissors, but Harrison and I counted eleven vegetable peelers one day.

Still, I like the Emerson house. For one thing, it's one of the only places in Sarah's Road that is far enough from Sarah's Road so you don't hear the road noises. But the best thing is Mr. Emerson doesn't mind if you make a mess. In fact, he acts like you couldn't possibly be having fun unless you have a chicken living in your kitchen and three or four projects going on in the living room. Whenever I start cleaning up, Mr. Emerson says, "Leave it, Ant. You and Harrison might want to get back to that tomorrow."

At my house the only place you're allowed to make

a mess is the backyard, and even then my mom will kill you if you don't clean up the second you're done. Harrison's house is a much better place to do projects, which is clearly what Harrison has in mind today.

"Okay, here's what we need to do . . . ," Harrison says when we are sitting cross-legged on his brown corduroy bedspread. "We've got to write her a note saying we're sorry—"

"I'm not sorry, though."

"Yes, you are." He gets Pistachio, who has made a spot for himself between us.

"I am?"

He nods so hard, I can hear his hair move.

I sigh. He's right. I am sorry. I didn't want to mess up Zoo Teens, that's for sure. It was so much fun taking care of the animals with Just Carol. But now everything is all screwed up. There seems no point in trying so hard about this. "She's never going to let me come back to the zoo, Harrison."

"Yes, she is. All you have to do is promise never to bring Tashi again. You can leave him over here if you're worried about his pills. My dad will give them to him." He touches Tashi lightly, the way you touch the frosting on a cake when you don't want to leave a mark. Pistachio licks Harrison's bitten-up fingernails.

"You need to eat corn, Ant."

"What?"

"You know, say you were wrong and you made a mistake."

"Oh. Crow. Eat crow, not corn."

Harrison crinkles up his nose. "Whatever." He

scratches at his chest. "We'll make a card. A very big card and . . . we need food."

"Food?"

He nods. "If you want to change somebody's mind, you got to bake them stuff. Pie, I think. And I'm going to draw the card. It's going to be this big." He puts his arms as wide as they will go. "You're going to write the inside. This will take care of everything."

I smile at this. Harrison thinks he can fix anything. He thinks he's Superman, behind all that hair.

"What am I going to write?" I ask as I scratch Pistachio under his chin. He lifts his head so I can do a better job and rests his little jaw on my hand.

"My dad will help us with the pie," Harrison says, which doesn't answer my question.

He hands me a paper and one of his pencils. "Now get busy!" He shakes his finger at me. Harrison is never like this at school.

I take the pencil and look at it. It's all nicked up with teeth marks, but the end is sharpened to a fine point, just the way Harrison likes it.

Harrison has a big stack of poster board. He runs his fingers over each piece, looking for bumps, creases, and wrinkles. Harrison is very particular about paper. When he settles on the piece he wants, he cuts the board in half with a razor blade and a ruler.

"It has to be real skinny," he explains to me. "Because I'm going to do a giraffe."

"What if I just write I'm sorry really tall to fill up the inside?"

Harrison's eyebrows slide up his brow. "I'm sorry is not enough," he says.

I sigh and begin writing while Harrison blocks in his giraffe. I love to watch him do this. He starts out by drawing a bunch of circles and squares that don't look like a giraffe at all, but when he puts them all together they look exactly like a giraffe. It's magic the way Harrison draws.

I settle down and try to write something that Harrison will think is okay. I do the best I can. "Okay, I'm done."

"Good," he says. "I need your help."

Harrison doesn't let me help with his drawings very often. And when he does, I get the easy parts, like filling in bricks or blades of grass or sky. Even so, I can't do as well as he does. But I love when he asks me to help. He doesn't care if I do it perfect, either. He says drawings don't look right if they're too perfect.

Now we are both lying on our bellies, drawing. Pistachio is curled up against my foot. Harrison is working on a leg and I'm doing clouds. I try to make them all light and swirly the way Harrison showed me, but mine don't swirl right. They look heavy enough to fall out of the sky and knock the giraffe out cold.

After we've been working for a while, Mr. Emerson knocks on the door frame. It's open, but he still knocks. Something about this reminds me of how much I like the Emersons and then I get a little panicky inside. I shouldn't get attached and I know it. If you get attached, then it hurts too much when you have to move away.

"Come in," Harrison says.

"I'm taking banana nut bread out of the oven in ten minutes. You want to take a break and get a piece while it's hot?"

My mouth waters. I'm about to say yes, when Harrison says, "Not now. We're busy." I rap Harrison with my pencil. He ignores me.

"You guys sure have been quiet up here. What are you working on?"

"We're making a giraffe card. And could you help with the pie?" Harrison squints through his crazy hair.

His father just finished baking banana nut bread. He's not going to want to bake a pie. "Maybe we could just bring her some banana bread," I suggest.

"Oh no," Harrison says. He pushes his hair out of his face. "It's got to be pie. When you make a mistake you have to give pie."

"Pie?" Mr. Emerson asks. He straightens up. His eyes get bright. He looks the way my father does when he runs his hand over his golf clubs. This surprises me. Then I remember, Mr. Emerson loves to cook.

"A mistake pie," Harrison says.

"Oh, I know." Mr. Emerson sits down on the brown beanbag chair in Harrison's room. "Humble pie."

"Yeah." Harrison smiles. "That's the one. What flavor is that?"

"Well, gee, guys." Mr. Emerson strokes his upper lip. "I don't know if there is a flavor for humble pie.

What are we sorry for? Maybe we should start with that."

"Will you read what you wrote?" Harrison asks me.

I shake my head no. I pretend to be shy, but this isn't it. I hate when Mr. Emerson finds out I messed up on something. I just hate it.

Harrison's tongue pokes at his cheek. He scratches his head. "We've got to get an adult opinion. We've got to, Ant. My dad will tell us if it's okay."

I sigh loud and long and roll my eyes. Pistachio groans and walks stiff legged over to Mr. Emerson, waggling his short tail. I read: "I am very sorry. I won't ever bring Pistachio to the zoo again. I didn't want him to get hurt. I only brought him because I was looking after him, but I guess this backfired. I know you want me to be honest and I will try. Just like George Washington. Except I don't know if he was honest or not. You know, that story about how he chopped down the cherry tree and then someone asked him and he said he couldn't lie that yes he did chop the tree down. I heard *that* is a big fat lie. I heard somebody made that all up. I think they're right, too, because why would George Washington chop down a cherry tree? Even back then there must have been way more fun things to do."

14
HUMBLE PIE

The card is too tall to fit into Harrison's locker, so Harrison bends it over a little, without making a crease, and slides it in that way. The pie we made is French apple and it fits fine on the shelf once Harrison moves his history book. The pie smells great. It has made his whole locker smell like cinnamon and brown sugar. I am unhappy that we have to give the whole thing away, but Harrison says not to be a baby about it. "This is serious, Ant. Kigali might not get fed without me."

I feel like telling him this is ridiculous and he knows it. But the giraffe Harrison drew is so beautiful, it looks like if you touch it, you'll feel giraffe hair instead of paper. One look at that drawing and anyone can tell how much Harrison loves Kigali already. Harrison can fall in love faster than anyone I know.

After lunch we find Just Carol searching for marker tops in the supply closet next to the office. She is so busy, she doesn't see us. Harrison and I stand there looking at each other, until she notices us.

"Well, hello," Just Carol says as her thumb clicks a red top on a red marker.

We stand awkwardly with the pie and the card. Harrison nudges me with his elbow.

"We have something to give you," I say. I hand her the pie. Harrison turns the card so she can see it.

Just Carol sets the pie down on a stack of green paper and stares at the card. She sucks air in, the way people do when they think you're about to do something dangerous.

"Oh, Harrison, it's beautiful! Absolutely exquisite. Did you do this all from your head?"

Harrison nods.

"You are amazing!" Just Carol shakes her head. "What a delicate hand. Unbelievable! It looks just like Kigali, too. Though you did take a couple of years off her, which was kind of you. When I'm old, I'm gonna get you to do my portrait." Just Carol rumples Harrison's already-rumpled hair. "I hope you're going to let me display this. Please say you will," Just Carol asks. She is all bubbly, her green eyes clear and full.

Normally, Harrison hates having his work tacked to a bulletin board or put in a glass case. I don't know why. He likes when people say nice things about his work, but it embarrasses him, too. He's funny that way. But now he is nodding, although his face is bright red, the color of the marker in Just Carol's hand. When I see this, I remember how once I saw him write Mrs. Carol Emerson under a picture he drew of Just Carol.

"Could we go back to the zoo with you? Ant's

sorry. Aren't you, Ant? She helped with the card, too. Read what she wrote," Harrison mumbles. I can hardly understand him. The end-of-lunch bell rings loud in my ear.

"Yes," I say, "I am sorry." This sounds fake, as if I'm reading a line in a book.

Just Carol's mouth forms a grim line.

Harrison clears his throat. "Have a piece of pie," he says, more clearly this time.

She ignores the pie, as if this is my contribution and she doesn't want any part of it. "Harrison, I'll take you to the zoo, but I can't take Ant."

I pucker my lips together and raise my eyes at Harrison. He nods toward Just Carol, like I'm supposed to say something.

"I made a mistake. I'm sorry." I point to the inside where I've written my bit. She reads it. Her expression doesn't change. There are a lot of kids in the hall now, hurrying to their classrooms. Just Carol looks as if she's finished talking.

"Mistakes happen," I say, loud so she'll hear over the noise of kids talking, "to everyone."

Just Carol closes the card. "Come on back to room 10. We'll talk for a minute," Just Carol says. Her eyes avoid me. She gathers her stack of green paper and three boxes of markers and fast walks down the corridor to the empty room 10. She sets her supplies and the card down and sits on the table. I like that she does this, because I know Mr. Borgdorf wouldn't. My mom wouldn't, either. "Chairs are for sitting. Tables are for working," she always says.

"What concerns me," Just Carol says when we are sitting down, too, "isn't the mistake, it's the deception. You hid that dog in your pocket."

"I always keep him in my pocket. How was I supposed to know it was against the rules to bring a dog to the zoo?"

"I find that hard to believe."

I look over at Harrison. He's biting his bottom lip. He runs his finger over initials carved into the desk. Something about the way he does this reminds me how much this means to him. "Well, I didn't tell you just in case it was against the rules," I say.

"Just in case," Just Carol says.

"Uh-huh." I try to look earnest.

"See, this is just the problem." Just Carol raps the eraser end of a yellow pencil on the desk. "I'm always in the position of trying to figure out whether or not you're telling the truth. And I will not be put in that position. You either tell me the truth, or I won't have anything to do with you."

"She will," Harrison mumbles.

Just Carol looks at Harrison for a long time. I don't think she wants to hurt his feelings any more than I do. "*If*, and I do mean *if*, you want to continue with Zoo Teens, you need to do two things." She raises two fingers. "One, you need to promise me that you will never lie or try to deceive me again. No direct lies—not even small ones. No indirect lies or deceptions like hiding Pistachio in your pocket. Do you understand what I'm saying?"

I nod.

"And two, you need to straighten out that vet problem."

"What vet problem?"

"Come on, Ant." Just Carol folds her arms in front of her and sets her elbows on the desk. Her green eyes won't let me go. "You know exactly what I'm talking about."

"How can I straighten it out? I don't have the money to pay!"

"I'm sure we can work that out. But we'll need to talk to your mom about it."

"My mom? Why do we have to bring her into this?"

"Because what you did was illegal. And she is the person responsible for you."

I look over at Harrison. He's nodding his head.

I take a deep breath. I suppose with Just Carol, I could maybe try the truth, kind of like an experiment. Maybe. But not with my mom. Please, not with my mom. Lies are the only way I can handle her.

I feel trapped. It's stuffy in this classroom and full of a dusty, chalky smell, which makes me cough. I want to get out.

"Look, Ant, your mom is going to find out about the vet one way or another. It will be better if you tell her."

"Better than what?" I ask, staring at the chalkboard, which has a list of things Columbus brought to America. Nutmeg, silk, cinnamon, salt, it says.

"Better than if she finds out from someone else."

I glare at Harrison. "See! I tell her one thing and she blabs it to everyone."

"I don't mean I'm going to report this or tell your

mom anything. I'm not. All I'm saying is, if you want to continue with the zoo program, this is what you need to do. If you don't, it's up to you how you want to deal with the vet. But I suspect that eventually the vet will track you down . . ." She cocks her head. "Or *the police.*"

"But they might not," I say. I look around the room. Anywhere but at Just Carol. My eyes rest on an overhead projector with its cord rolled in a neat stack of O's.

"That's true, but if you do it again, the odds are you'll be found."

"Who says I'm going to do it again?"

"I'm hoping you don't. But I see the way you love that dog, and I suspect that if he gets sick again, you'll take him to the vet."

"I'll go to a different vet, that's all." I look out the window as a group of fourth-grade girls walk by.

"There aren't that many vets. And who knows if the next one will insist on payment when services are rendered. That's typically the way it works, you know."

She has me now. I've thought of this before. I've wondered what I would do if I had to take Pistachio in again. There are four other veterinary hospitals in the Yellow Pages, but they are a long way away.

Harrison has a pencil in his hand. He has erased half of a car somebody else drew on the desk. Now he is redrawing it, much better this time.

"So if we tell her about the last time, what does that have to do with the next time?"

"I don't want to promise anything, Ant. But I will

talk to your mom about working out a way for you to take Pistachio to the vet when he needs to go." She looks over at Harrison. "Do we have a deal?"

I say nothing. The late bell rings. "I'll be at your house tonight, okay, Ant?"

Harrison kicks me under the desk.

I look out to the now quiet hall. The lights are buzzing in this room. It sounds like a thousand tiny grasshoppers are trapped inside. But I am nodding. I am.

15
JUST CAROL

I watch out the window for Just Carol. Pistachio sits in my lap. I told my mom Just Carol was coming, but I didn't exactly explain why. "She wants to talk to you about the zoo program," I said. "Oh," my mother replied, and that was it. She's preoccupied today. I don't know why.

I try to imagine what will happen when Just Carol gets here. Part of me wants my mother to behave badly in front of Just Carol. I think Just Carol will like me better if my mother is mean. No one would love Cinderella if she didn't have a mean stepmom. The other part of me wants Just Carol to wave a wand over my mother and change her into the mom I want. A mom who says, "You know, I'm sorry. If I had let you take Pistachio to the vet in the first place, none of this would have happened." I think about my real mother. This is exactly what she would say.

I sit there fretting and watching the driveway. My tummy gurgles, the way it does when I get upset. Then, without thinking about it, I do something I almost never do. I dial the number on the kitchen bulletin board. The one beside "Don/Atlanta Office."

My dad will be mad, but right now, I don't care. I mean, if Elizabeth can call him, why can't I? This way he can talk to Just Carol on the phone, and my mom won't have to know anything about it. When Just Carol comes, I'll just hand her the phone and she won't have to see my mom at all. My dad doesn't get so upset about stuff like this. Once when I was little, I bit Felicia Johnston's arm because she cut a big handful of Elizabeth's hair, and when my dad found out, he was almost proud of what I'd done.

I wind the phone cord around my finger and wait for the call to connect. "Leebson Insurance," the receptionist says.

"Could I speak to Don MacPherson, please?"

"I'm sorry, Don MacPherson is no longer with the company. Could someone else in our sales department help you?"

"What?"

"Mr. MacPherson no longer works for Leebson."

My mouth opens. Nothing comes out.

"Miss? Hello?" The receptionist asks, "Can someone else help you?"

"No," I say. I hang up the phone. Pistachio squirms against me. It takes me a while to realize I'm holding him too tight.

The receptionist is wrong. That's all there is to it. I stand staring stupidly at "Don/Atlanta Office" written in my mother's neat handwriting. Then, my feet walk up the stairs to Elizabeth's room. I'm not quite sure why they do this except that I know Elizabeth hates moving as much as I do. It's the one thing we agree on, Elizabeth and me.

Elizabeth has scooted her chair up to her dresser. Her nose is two inches from the mirror. She is inspecting her chin. "Elizabeth," I say, "I called the Atlanta office. The receptionist said Dad's not working at Leebson anymore."

I can almost see the words travel inside Elizabeth's head and register in her eyes. Her eyelids close, her head rocks back.

"She's probably wrong," I say. "It's probably a mistake."

Elizabeth shakes her head. "Must have just happened. I've been calling every week to check."

"You have? Why?"

"Because I knew this was going to happen, that's why."

"Oh," I say. Elizabeth has been checking up on our dad. This is not what I wanted to hear. I feel as if Elizabeth has just belted me in the gut. I take a deep breath and try to recover. This feels even worse than the receptionist saying he doesn't work at Leebson. It feels more real, somehow.

Elizabeth sits absolutely still for a minute, then jumps to her feet and runs down the stairs. I follow her out to the backyard, where my mother is tugging a weed vine that has snaked itself around her yellow pansies.

"MOM, DID DAD QUIT?" Elizabeth cries.

My mother's head snaps up, her hand is gripping the vine. Her eyes look surprised and unhappy, like she's just spilled grape juice on herself.

When I see this, I know it's true. I try to carve a way this will all be okay. Maybe he already has a new job right here. Maybe that's why he quit.

"How did you find that out?" my mother asks just as the doorbell chimes its fake-organ sound.

"He better get a new job in Sarah's Road, because I'm not leaving. *I'm not!*" Elizabeth says, her voice low and tough.

"Me neither. There's no way," I say. "Where is Dad if he's not in Atlanta?"

My mother shakes her head and bites her bottom lip.

"Mom, where is he?" Elizabeth asks.

The doorbell chimes again.

"He's in Philadelphia visiting Uncle Anthony. Now who is that?" she asks, wiping her hands on a yellow plaid dishrag she keeps in her gardening pants pocket.

"Just Carol," I say.

"Why did he quit?" Elizabeth asks.

"Look, I'm not going to play middleman here. He's calling tonight. You talk to him about this, not me," she tells Elizabeth, then turns to me. "Antonia, are you in trouble again?"

I shrug my shoulders. My mom's hands fly to her head to push a loose strand of hair behind her ear. She has a pained expression on her face. "I am in no mood for this," she says.

"I mean it, Mom," Elizabeth says.

"Enough, Elizabeth. You've made your point. We'll talk about this later."

I give my mom a comfortable lead as she walks through the house to the front door. I don't want her to notice I have Pistachio and tell me to put him outside. I can't face this without him.

"Hello, Mrs. MacPherson. I'm very sorry to intrude," Just Carol says when my mom opens the door. Just Carol is smiling hard, in a funny no-teeth-showing way.

Kate is in the living room watching TV. The doorbell rings loudest in the living room, but she probably didn't hear it. Kate watches TV the way she counts money. If a stack of nickels is in front of her, she can't see anything else.

"Kate, you're going to have to turn that off," my mother says. Kate's whole face gets red, and she looks as if she might explode. The only time Kate ever gets mad at my mother is when my mother makes her turn the TV off. "Katherine." My mom whispers something in her ear. Kate calms down. She still looks grumpy, but not like she's ready to kill. She heaves a couple of times, then presses the power off. In the sudden silence, Kate's trance is broken and she looks over at Just Carol.

"You're the art lady for the upper grades," Kate says.

"Yes, I am." Just Carol smiles.

Kate settles into the sofa as if she's going to stay.

"Kate," my mom says, "would you go upstairs, please, honey."

Kate smiles sweetly at my mom. "Yes, Mommy," Kate says. She walks by me. I hear the coins jingle in her shoe. "What did you do now?" She mouths the words at me.

"So," my mother says when Kate is upstairs, "what is this all about?" My mother is being very polite, but she has her guard up. Her mouth is smiling a pretend smile. She is standing up and hasn't suggested any of us might sit down.

"Ant has something to tell you," Just Carol says.

"Antonia," my mother says.

"Antonia, yes," Just Carol corrects herself.

My mother is staring at me now. Her mouth is not smiling, not even in a pretend way.

I look up at Kate, who is crouched by the upstairs banister, trying to hear every word. "I took Pistachio to the vet," I say. I look down at him. He tries to wiggle out of my arms. The sound of our voices is making him nervous. Or maybe it's just that he knows he isn't supposed to be in the living room.

My mother waits for more.

"I took Pistachio to the vet and I didn't pay for it," I say.

"How much?" my mother asks. She sits down. Just Carol and I sit down, too.

"I don't know," I say.

"You don't know, or you don't want to tell me?"

"I don't know."

Just Carol clears her throat. Her green eyes laser through my head.

"I gave the vet the wrong address, so you won't get

a bill." I look down at the rug. I wish I could crawl under it. This didn't seem like such a terrible thing when I did it. It certainly didn't seem like stealing. It seemed like taking care of my dog. But now with Just Carol and my mother staring at me, I feel like I wet my bed.

"The vet on the corner of Deeson and Meyer Way?"

"No. I went to a new one."

My mother snorts. "And why are you telling me this?" She looks at Just Carol.

"Because Just Carol says I have to straighten this out, otherwise I can't go to the zoo anymore." I pet Tashi, hoping my mom doesn't tell me to take him out of here.

My mother nods her head. Her tongue rolls over her teeth.

"So it wasn't your idea to tell me, it was Miss Carol's."

I look down at Pistachio.

"You're the art teacher?" my mother says.

"Yes."

"So what are you suggesting?" my mother asks Just Carol.

"I think you and Antonia need to go to the vet and find out how much is owed and then figure out a way for Antonia to work it off. And I think"—Just Carol is looking shaky now—"you need to work out an arrangement for vet care for her dog. Because I feel like this is going to happen again unless Ant—Antonia can feel as if she is taking responsible care of Pistachio."

"*Responsible* care," my mother says. She has been

fairly calm until now, but this last statement seems to have irked her. "And tell me how this has anything to do with the business of art?"

"It's only my business because Antonia told me about it."

"So you've come here to tell me I'm a bad mother and I've made bad decisions."

"Not at all, Mrs. MacPherson."

"Sure you are," my mother says, taking a Kleenex from her pocket and blowing her nose. My mother is the only person I know who can blow her nose this delicately. The rest of the world honks away, but she sniffles sweetly and politely. I don't see how she can get her snot out this way.

"That's what you were saying with that trip to the principal's office. You were saying I am such a bad mother that my child wants a new one. As if I didn't know she had this whole adoption fantasy going. You were trying to rub my nose in it, but luckily your principal saw through you."

"I can see how you could feel that way." Just Carol is focusing all the intensity of her green eyes on my mother. "I'm sorry I handled that the way I did."

This stops my mother. She seems surprised that Just Carol has said this. She takes a breath and starts again. "And as for Pistachio, Pistachio is old. And if Antonia had her way, that dog would be going to the vet twice a week. I mean, what can a vet do about old age? Or is this my fault, too?"

"I'm not trying to make any of this your fault," Just Carol says.

"I don't take him every week. I only take him when he's sick," I say.

"Well, perhaps we could start a vet fund. And Antonia could do some extra work in order to have enough money to take him when you both decide he needs it." Just Carol looks at me and then at my mom.

"Are you a new teacher?" my mom asks.

"I've been teaching for two years."

"That's not a very long time."

"No, it isn't."

"Look, I know you're trying to help Antonia, but I can't help thinking you're going about it the wrong way," my mom says.

I look at my mom. I can see how hard she's trying to control herself.

"You may be right. But I've made a promise to your daughter that if she takes care of this vet bill problem, she will be able to continue with the zoo program, and I'd like to be able to keep that commitment. But I think she needs your help to resolve some of these issues."

"Why are you sticking your neck out for her?"

"Because I like her," Just Carol says.

My lips smile. I feel a warm flush come over me. For a second I'm afraid I might cry. I wonder if Kate heard this. I hope she did. I hope she tells Elizabeth about it, too.

My mother looks at me as if she's trying to understand why. She's quiet for a minute, then she nods. Her head barely moves. "I do fine with the other two," she says softly. "I've never been called on the carpet about them."

"Mrs. MacPherson, please, I'm not calling you on the carpet. It's just that we have a problem, and I think we need to address it."

"With Antonia everything is a problem."

"Antonia, why don't you go upstairs. I want to talk to your mom for a minute, alone," Just Carol says.

I shake my head no in an exaggerated way. "I don't think that's a good idea," I whisper.

"I do," Just Carol says. There's an edge to the way she says this. Like if you touched her words, they would give you a paper cut. I go upstairs.

Kate is sitting on the top step. "You're not supposed to take Pistachio in the living room," Kate says. She has her notebook in her hand as if she has already recorded this. "And I don't see how you could get in trouble in art. How can you do *art* wrong?"

"I didn't get in trouble in art," I say.

"What did you do, then?" She leans forward. Her mouth open. Her blue eyes glowing.

"None of your business," I say as I close the door of my room.

16
NOSE

Now I'm dialing Just Carol's number wanting her to answer for once, instead of that tape machine I've heard so often. Nope, it's the machine again. I hang up without leaving a message and then I sit, staring at nothing. If I don't care about her one way or the other, why do I call her so much?

My mother is in the garage. She is opening old packed boxes. I hear the blade of her scissors cut the brown tape, then the rip of cardboard as she pulls open the flaps. She is checking to see if she still wants what's inside. I go in the living room to put on a CD and drown the sound out. Your Highness beats me to it. Neither of us can stand the sound of my mom cleaning the garage, because we know it means she thinks we'll be moving soon. We remember the last time and the time before that.

Now it's almost time for my father to call. He is supposed to phone at 7:30. I check the clock in the kitchen. It's 7:15 every time I look. Finally it moves— 7:18. The phone rings. I get the downstairs extension. Elizabeth rips it out of my hand.

"Dad!" I hear Elizabeth say as I run for the upstairs phone. "You're not looking for a job in Philadelphia, are you?"

"What about hello? Don't we usually start with that?"

"Antonia called Leebson in Atlanta. They said you weren't working there anymore."

"Oh, she did, did she."

"Yes, I did," I say.

"Hello, Antonia."

"Dad. We have to stay *here*, you know. You can't get a job in Pennsylvania."

"No hello. No how are you. You girls arc a tough crowd, I'm telling you. But in answer to your question, No, I'm not looking for a job in Philadelphia. Happy now?"

"Why'd you leave?" Elizabeth asks.

"I gave my notice at Leebson because it was time. I had planned to stay there until they found a replacement, but my crazy ex-boss, Dave, got so upset he told me to pack my desk and get out. It's just as well. It wasn't the right place for me. This is a very positive move."

"Why didn't you tell us?" I ask.

"You didn't give me time."

"Fine, Dad, but we're not moving," Elizabeth says.

"Boy, are you two feisty today. Settle down, okay? There's nothing to worry about."

"But where are you going to work now?" Elizabeth asks.

"Elizabeth, it's been seventy-two hours—eighty

maybe—since I left the last job. I don't know yet where I'm going to be working. But I'm not planning on moving you to Siberia, I promise. Of course, I'll try to stay in northern California. I know you girls like it there and so does your mother."

"You'll *try*?" I say.

"Yes, I'll try. Now put your mom on. I'm tired of getting the third degree."

"You have to do better than that," Elizabeth says.

"ELIZABETH! Don't talk to me that way! Now get your mom, please!"

I put the phone down. I don't want to hear any more. Elizabeth comes upstairs. Kate follows. She has heard what happened, but she doesn't totally get it. She still trusts my parents in a way Elizabeth and I do not.

I don't know what Elizabeth and I thought we'd get from talking to my dad. But whatever it is, we didn't get it. We waited for nothing. No information. Zip.

We sit down in the doorways of our rooms. This is neutral zone. Elizabeth rolls a pink rubber ball to me. I roll it to Kate. Kate rolls it to Elizabeth. We listen to my mom speak to my dad on the phone—a distant talking sound, rising and falling. It stops after a few minutes. Fewer than normal.

We are like zombies hypnotized by that ball, rolling it back and forth. Back and forth. After a while, my mother walks by with a load of laundry. I'm happy to see this. The laundry is an ordinary chore, nothing to do with moving.

My mom steps over Elizabeth, then stops. It's un-heard of for the three of us to be doing something together. My mother seems to notice this. "So, what are you playing?" she asks.

"Nothing," Elizabeth says. Elizabeth's head is rocking as if she's keeping beat to a song that only she hears. She does this when she's upset. My mother watches Elizabeth. She waits for more. Elizabeth is staring at the ball as if stopping it with her hand and rolling it to me requires all her concentration. "We're playing with a pink ball," she replies.

"I can see that," my mom says as she sets a stack of neatly folded laundry on Elizabeth's bed.

My mom comes out of Elizabeth's room and goes into Kate's. When she passes by again, Elizabeth says, "We don't want to move."

"Your dad didn't say we were moving," my mom says, running her manicured nails through her neatly curled blond hair.

"He's got to get a new job now. You know what that means," Elizabeth says. She is still concentrating on the ball. Her head is down, her blond ballerina bun is up. Usually Elizabeth is pretty neat, too, but today her hair is falling out of her bun and she is wearing sweat shorts with holes in them. Her fair skin is blotchy, like it gets when she's been crying.

"There are plenty of jobs around here, you know," my mom says. She tries to say this in a matter-of-fact way. But the words wobble when they come out.

"See," Kate says. "Didn't I tell you?"

Elizabeth rolls her eyes.

"There always are plenty of jobs, but Dad never takes them. He takes the ones that mean we have to move one thousand miles or more and miss my per-formances," Elizabeth whispers, staring hard at the ground.

"What?" my mother asks.

"There is no way I can leave, Mom. You know that," Elizabeth says, loud now, so my mother can hear. Elizabeth has the ball and she's bouncing it low and hard like a basketball dribble. "I absolutely can't. I'm going to be in *The Nutcracker* this year. Don't you even remember that?"

"For goodness' sakes . . . no one is asking you to give up *The Nutcracker*. Didn't your dad say he'd try to find a job here? What else can he do?" my mother asks. This is her I-don't-want-to-hear-any-more-about-it tone of voice. It's surprising to hear her speak this way to Elizabeth. I am happy to hear it . . . thrilled, ac-tually. But then I start thinking about Harrison and Mr. Emerson and Just Carol and all the things I'll lose if we move and the happiness fades away.

"Why are you cleaning out the garage, then?" I ask.

"Because it's dirty," my mother says.

"You're not going to get us up in the middle of the night, are you?" Elizabeth asks. Her voice is soft now. She is scared.

"Elizabeth, I don't know where you get these ideas. It was a vacation. We got you up in the middle of the night because we were driving across the desert and it was too hot to go in the day. What has gotten into you?" she asks, picking up her empty plastic laundry basket. She shakes her head and mutters, "You're starting to sound like Antonia."

"What?" Elizabeth asks.

"Never mind," my mother says, and then she is gone down the stairs.

"I am not going to leave," Elizabeth says when we hear the kitchen door swing behind my mother.

"I'm not going to leave, either," I say.

"They can't make us," Elizabeth announces. Refusing to do things is unusual for Elizabeth. Generally, she gets what she wants in a sneakier way.

"Sure they can. They can make us do anything they want," I say. I have had a lot more experience with disobedience. This is my area of expertise.

"We could run away," Elizabeth says, her blue eyes all lit up in her blotchy face.

I snort. "Elizabeth, they don't have street shelters with pink canopy beds, you know."

"Shut up, Ant," Elizabeth says.

I'm surprised to hear her call me Ant. It makes me happy, even if it is preceded by "shut up." I look at her. I have never seen her so unhappy. She is rocking back and forth and tears are spilling over her eyelids and running down her cheeks.

I bite my lip. I'm not quite sure what to do now. It seems weird for Elizabeth and me to both be mad at our mom.

"Antonia, did you leave this mess down here?" my mom calls up the stairs.

"Better go down." Elizabeth nods toward Mom.

Usually, Elizabeth and Kate love when I get in trouble. They eat it up. Right after my mother gets mad at me, they run around helping her do chores for a while just to prove how much better they are than me. But today, Elizabeth doesn't seem to want me to be in trouble.

"I didn't leave the mess," I tell Elizabeth.

"Yes, you did. It's from when you brushed Pistachio."

"Oh. Maybe I did." I smile.

"Antonia!" my mother calls louder this time.

I shake my head and get up.

Elizabeth has the ball stopped with one hand. "She doesn't hate you as much as you think she does, you know," Elizabeth says.

I am surprised to hear Elizabeth say this. She has never said anything like it before. In fact, usually she says just the opposite.

"But you sure do make her mad. Especially when you tell her that she isn't your real mother. Man oh man. You might as well pour gasoline on her and strike a match."

"Well, she isn't," I say.

"Oh, come on, Ant. Just because you don't like our mom doesn't mean you can make up a new one." She shakes her head.

"She's your mom. She isn't mine. For one thing, in case you haven't noticed, I don't look at all like her," I say.

"Not now, but she looked like you when she was a kid, before she got her nose fixed and her hair permed and dyed."

When Elizabeth says this, I feel a sharp pain in my chest.

"No, she didn't," I say, but it's too late, because suddenly I see a photo in my mind. It is in Aunt Mindy's house, on the dresser in Aunt Mindy's bedroom. The picture is of Aunt Mindy and my mom when they were little girls. They are wearing matching dresses with white sailor collars. They are both petting a big orange cat. Aunt Mindy looks like herself, only younger. My mom looks like me.

17
OTHER DOGS' STINK

Dear Real Mom,
Okay, so you aren't real. Okay, so I've known this all along. Big deal. I'm going to believe in you just the same. Because I am not Mrs. MacPherson's daughter. I'm not. Lots of people look alike and they aren't related. They do. And Pistachio isn't their dog, either. I know this for a fact.

Sincerely,
Ant and Pistachio

Every day for the past two weeks I've been going home to get Pistachio and then walking to the vet's office to work. Mostly I clean the kennels in the back. I use this stinky green stuff and a big yellow scrub brush. It isn't fun. Especially since they take the dogs and cats away, so I don't even get to pet them or talk to them or anything. The vet has made it clear I'm being punished. She doesn't like me. I don't like her, either, but the receptionist with the fluffy white dog is very nice. I can tell she doesn't think what I did was all that bad. I'll bet she believes in the Hippopotamus oath, too.

At least the vet lady lets me bring Pistachio. I made a bed for him out of an old blue blanket, but he hardly ever lies in it because of all the smells. He just can't get enough of smelling other dogs' stink. The only thing he doesn't like is the smelly green soap. When I squirt it in the bucket, he curls his lip and shakes his head and backs away. I don't blame him. I hate it, too. It makes me feel as if I'm about to sneeze. Like I say "Aah aah aah," but never "Choo."

The other things I hate are the creepy purple pamphlets. They are in the brochure rack along with some other colored papers about fleas and heartworm and housebreaking. Or they were, anyway. Now the purple pamphlets are in the Dumpster underneath a big load of dog poop. That is where they belong. They are trash. Worse than trash, really. On the cover is a picture of a sad old golden retriever and a badly drawn clock. The words are printed in computer handwriting. They say: "Is it time to euthanize?" What they really mean is: "Are you ready to butcher your best friend?" Only if they said that and had a picture of a person there, they'd get arrested.

That clock really gets me. It reminds me of the homework pages Kate got when she was in first grade. The ones where she had to draw in the hands of the clock to show: breakfast time, lunchtime, dinnertime. And now: slaughter time.

I never even read the inside of the pamphlet. The cover is enough to tell me that I would never take Pistachio to this vet again. I don't care that I am supposed to be earning money toward future vet care for him. I'd rather go to jail than take him to a vet who would have a pamphlet like that. I keep my eye out for them now, and when I see one, I take it straight to the Dumpster in the alley out back.

The way I figure it, this is my good deed for the day. It's a lot more important than cleaning the kennels. Still, cleaning the kennels is what lets me go to the zoo with Harrison on Saturdays. And this is really fun. The other good thing is, because I'm always at the vet or at the zoo, I haven't been around my mom much lately. And when I am home, my mother acts funny toward me. She doesn't forget I'm there the way she used to. She watches me and she asks a lot of questions about Just Carol. "What do you think that teacher of yours would say about this?" she asks when she catches me sneaking down the back trellis with Pistachio in my pocket. "How should I know?" I say.

One day she asked, "So, what does that teacher of yours have to say about me?"

"About you? Just Carol doesn't say anything about you," I tell her, but she acts like this couldn't possibly be true, like I'm holding back. I'm not holding back. I do like that what Just Carol thinks seems to matter to her, though. It makes me feel safer somehow, as if my mother no longer has the final say on everything.

My biggest problem is still my dad. Elizabeth drew him a map and highlighted in pink all the places he could work around here, but I wonder if he'll pay any attention. He says he will, but then he has this habit of "forgetting." When my dad says he doesn't remember, it makes me so frustrated I could scream, because there's nothing I can say to that. Forgetting is an easy loophole. A weasel route out of trouble. Forgetting is worse than lying. That's why I'm glad for the map. It's all on paper now. We taped it to my dad's briefcase, so it will be hard for him to "forget."

The other problem is Harrison. He is acting funny about this Math-a-thon thing. First he said he couldn't possibly come because the Math-a-thon is Saturday and that's when we usually go to the zoo. Then, when he found out Just Carol was coming to the Math-a-thon, so for sure there would be no zoo that day, he got very quiet. I hate when he does this. If I didn't know him so well, I'd think he was being mean. But I know with Harrison that's never it. Harrison is never mean.

Today when I see him, he's sitting on the ground outside Spanish class. He's drawing, of course. Usually now he draws giraffes instead of chickens, but today he's back to a chicken drawing—one he started a long time ago. He is almost done. The only thing left is one chicken foot and part of the head. It is always amazing to me how he knows so clearly what chickens look like from every point of view. It's as if he has a CD-ROM full of chicken parts in his head.

"Why are you being weird about this Math-a-thon?" I ask him.

"Why are you going to it?"

This is a good question. I never really thought about why I agreed to go, except that it hadn't taken any effort so far and Cave Man said I should. But usually having a teacher say I ought to do something is all the reason I need to refuse.

I'm not sure what the real reason is. It may be because I want Just Carol to think I'm smart. Of course, it has occurred to me that she already thinks I'm smart, and if I crash and burn in the Math-a-thon, that will change her mind. But I don't think I will, because I'm good at math. I don't really try hard, either. It's like a part of my brain already knows how to solve the problems. The wrong ways and the right ways. I follow all the paths through to the end and back again.

One of the reasons I like math is because a right answer is right, no matter who grades your homework. In English, a teacher will give you a bad grade on a paper just because you have a big mouth or she doesn't like your handwriting. But in math, it's never like that.

I think about how to explain this to Harrison. Apparently he thinks this Math-a-thon is dangerous somehow, as if it's going to lead me someplace he can't follow. I can't get him to see how ridiculous this is. Last year, when I got sick to death of being sent to talk to Mr. Borgdorf and I started doing my work in class, he worried about that, too. But then he got used to it and it was okay. It's not as if Harrison likes to get in trouble. He doesn't. But he hates changes, and he worries school will get in the way of important things like his art and us being friends. Adults always act as if school is supposed to be more important than your friends, which Harrison and me think is just plain wrong. We've discussed this many times.

"I just want to," I say.

He chews his pencil and says nothing. I see this is not good enough.

"Maybe Just Carol has something to do with it," I say.

He puts his face back down next to his page and gets busy with his pencil. "You don't have to be good at math, you know."

"I know," I say. "It's like a puzzle, Harrison. I just want to know if I can do it."

"What if you can?"

I shrug. "So then I can."

"You going to start doing this on Saturdays instead of the zoo?"

"No. I love going to the zoo."

Harrison isn't drawing now. He's chomping on his pencil. His hair is in his face, I can't see his eyes.

"What if you like this math stuff better?"

"Harrison, I'm just going to try this. It's only one Saturday. People don't do this every Saturday."

"Are you going in a bus?"

"No."

"I'm not good at math. I couldn't go on a bus," Harrison says.

"There's no bus, Harrison. And so what if you're not good at math? I'm not good at drawing."

He nods. "Are you going to want to be friends with Keegan and Madison? They're good at math. They probably sit together on the bus."

"Harrison." I give his arm a gentle slap. "I'm not

going to be friends with Keegan and Madison and I'm not going anywhere on a bus. Are you friends with Sarah Feldman just because she's a good artist?"

"No. I'm friends with you."

"Yeah, and I'm friends with you, so don't get weird on me. Besides, maybe Just Carol will let us go to the zoo on Sunday this week. We could ask."

"Yeah, let's ask." He smiles his one-sided, one-dimpled smile. I still can't see his eyes. All I see is hair and mouth.

"So are you coming to the Math-a-thon? I need you."

Harrison pushes his hair out of his face and makes his eyes go crossways. Then he smiles back at me. "Okay, sure," he says.

18
A RIDE

My mother is all dressed up in her blue high heels with her only-for-special-occasions perfume on. I don't know why she's dressed this way. It's only Elizabeth's dress rehearsal, not even the real show or anything.

Elizabeth is wearing her good pink leotard and tights. Her hair is pulled back so tight it looks as if it is giving her a headache. Kate is wearing her pink leotard and her hair is slicked back, too, just like Elizabeth's. Kate is only going to dance class, but my mom let her get dressed up, too.

Dad got home last night. I can hear him in the shower. I am hanging outside his door, waiting for him to finish. Pistachio is nestled in the crook of my arm.

"How are you getting to your Math-a-thon, Antonia?" my mom asks as she floats by smelling like lavender.

"Just Carol is picking me up," I say. This is a lie—a dumb one, too. I should get a ride from my mom, but I want my dad to take me. Elizabeth has to be there early, so my mom is taking her. Probably my dad is going later when the performance starts. But maybe he's not. Maybe, if he gives me a ride, then he'll see what a big deal this Math-a-thon is and he'll stay and watch me—at least for part of it.

I wait until I hear my mom and Elizabeth and Kate get in the car, then I knock on the bathroom door. "Dad?"

"Yes?" his voice sounds slightly muffled through the door.

"Are you going to play golf today?"

"No."

"Oh." Pistachio wiggles in my arm. He wants to get down. I switch arms, hoping this will get him comfortable again.

"Are you going to do something else, then?" I wish he'd come out. It's impossible to talk through a closed door.

"Many other things. I've got a full plate today, then I'm flying to New York tomorrow. I have to pull together some documents and do a lot of—"

"NEW YORK!" I scream. The word roars in my ears. "YOU'RE NOT GOING TO GET A JOB IN NEW YORK?"

The lock pops, the knob turns, and I get a warm blast of steam when the door opens. My dad comes out, looking fresh, just out of the shower. His wet hair has comb marks and his skin is all pink. He smells of shampoo and toothpaste and soap and steam.

"Relax, Antonia. It's corporate headquarters. The job is here."

"Oh," I sigh. My dad walks into my parents' bedroom. I follow him. I don't think he'll say anything about Pistachio being in here. My mother would in a second, but my dad doesn't notice stuff like this.

"Are any of those things you have to do down Johnson Ranch Road?" I ask.

"No."

"What about if you decide to go to the driving range?"

"What is it you need, Antonia?" my father asks. He ducks down to see himself in the mirror on his dresser. Then he looks at me in the mirror.

"I'm going to the Math-a-thon, did Mom tell you?" I see the reflection of myself and my father.

He nods his head. "She mentioned it. Something about a postcard and some confusion about who was invited."

"Oh, I was hoping you'd give me a ride," I say. I want to ask him if he'll come. I want to tell him I'd really like it if he would, but I can't say this. It seems too personal. Too true. Besides, I can't stand it if he turns me down.

"A ride?" My dad spins around and looks at me. "Your mother drove right by there. Why didn't you go with her?"

I shrug and look down at my parents' dresser. A card and a rose are leaning against my mom's jewelry box. The card looks as if it came from Elizabeth. It has the slanty writing Elizabeth likes to do and a picture of a ballerina copied from a book. I pick it up. "You are cordially invited to a preview performance," it says. I hate Elizabeth. She always figures out how to get what she wants.

I take a deep breath. "Are you going to Elizabeth's dress rehearsal?" I ask.

"I sure hope so. I'm certainly going to try. I've got to stop by Kinko's first and I'm really hoping it doesn't take too long."

"So could I?" I ask, petting Pistachio's head.

"Could you what?" He's digging in his drawer for something.

"Have a ride?"

My father groans. His head shoots back, like someone slapped his face. "Antonia, why do you do this? It's as if you go out of your way to be annoying to your mother and me." He shakes his head. "I wasn't going that way. I wasn't leaving right now."

"Well, forget it, then," I say. I take Pistachio to my room and set him on the floor. Then I fill his bowl from my own private sink. For a second, I think about taking Tashi to the Math-a-thon. I would certainly like him to come with me, but it seems too hard to hide him. Besides, I don't feel like getting Just Carol upset all over again. Getting her un-upset was way too much trouble. "Bye, Tashi," I say, then I march into Elizabeth's room to get her helmet. I will just have to borrow her bike. That's all.

My father is downstairs reading the paper when I walk by on my way to the garage. "I suppose you're going to be late now," he says from behind his newspaper.

I ignore this and go into the garage to get Elizabeth's bike. I try to wheel it out from behind the boxes of stuff my mother is sorting through, but it won't go.

It has a flat tire and the chain has slipped off the gears.

My father opens the door and steps into the garage. He sees the flat tire. "Antonia." He shakes his head. "You have to learn to think ahead!"

This stings. I did think ahead. I thought this all out very carefully. If I'd asked him to come to the Math-a-thon last night, then my mom would have known I'd lied, plus I'd still have to compete with Elizabeth. My only chance was to wait until after my mom and Elizabeth left. I may be a liar, but I'm not stupid.

"C'mon," my father says. "Let's get going, I'm never going to make it to your sister's dress rehearsal at this rate. And your mother will have my head if I miss it."

I follow him to the car. We get in. He backs out, his hand over the seat looking behind him. I don't say a word as we drive to school.

My school is on a cul-de-sac and today it's clogged with traffic. Cars are trying to park, cars are dropping kids off, cars are turning around. Families are walking into the auditorium. People are everywhere. The marquee sign out front says District 2 Math-a-Thon. Welcome Contestants and Their Families.

I hope my dad will see this. I hope he will understand that not everybody is invited to be in the District 2 Math-a-thon. I want him to know this is a special thing. I want him to come in with me.

"Antonia, it looks like a real jam up there, they must be having a soccer game today. I'm going to let you out here, then I can duck down Rio Road and miss that whole mess."

"It's not a soccer game, it's a Math-a-thon."

He nods his head. "Come on, hop out. I'm blocking traffic. I got to scoot on out of here."

I don't move.

"Antonia!"

"Look, Dad, maybe I'll just stay with you today."

"With me? I'm going to Kinko's." My father's voice drops. His eyes move quickly back and forth as if he is looking for a way out. "I thought you wanted to go to this math-a-thing?"

I look out the window at my school. I'm suddenly afraid to get out. I want my dad to come with me. I want to hold his hand, the way I did when I was little.

The car behind us toots its horn.

"Antonia!" my dad cries.

"Forget it," I say. I get out, slam the door, and watch my dad pull away. The turn signal goes on. I watch the yellow orange flash flash. The car turns and he's gone.

19
THE MaTH-a-THon

I have never been to a Math-a-thon before. Cave Man told me how it works, though. He said they give each kid a problem and then they start a giant wall-size stopwatch. Whoever finishes the problem correctly before the buzzer buzzes goes to the next heat. Six kids from my class are in my section. Joyce Ann Jensen, Alexandra Duncan, Keegan and Madison and some other kids I don't know very well mainly because the smart kids don't hang around Harrison and me. In fact, Joyce Ann is staring at me now as if I am the last person in the world she expected to be here.

I look around for Harrison. I wish we'd come together. He should be here by now, because I'm so late that this lady in a blue dress is already herding sixth graders onto the auditorium stage, where twenty desks and chairs are set up. I file in behind Joyce Ann Jensen and choose a desk as far from the audience as possible. I sit down and rock back in my chair and make my eyes into slits, as if I couldn't care less about any stupid Math-a-thon. I don't want to test my brain against other kids. It reminds me of competing with

Elizabeth. Every time I'm up against her, I lose. And if I don't lose, everyone thinks I cheated. Harrison is right. I don't belong here.

I get up to leave, then I see Just Carol. She waves at me and I wave back. Then I do some lame made-up motions, as if I only stood up to stretch. I do this badly, like I am a close relation to Goofy.

Now, the answer lady in the blue dress starts talking about the rules. She is describing them in such detail she is making them twice as complicated as they really are. "In the event your pencil lead breaks or there's a disturbance such as a fire alarm blahblahblah . . ." Finally, she hands out the problems. Then I'm not nervous, I'm bored. It's so easy, a kindergartner could do it. I draw doodles on mine, because I am done way early. In fact, everybody finishes early, and by the time the buzzer goes off, the answer lady and her student helpers have already checked all the cards. Then the answer lady clicks on her microphone. "Excellent. 100 percent correct on the first heat. Ladies and gentlemen, let's give these kids a hand."

By the fourth round, things start to get interesting and we lose a few people. Now it takes me the whole time to get the answer right, and I'm wishing I never agreed to do this. Why did I, anyway? Maybe, after this round, I should drop out. I don't really know how smart I am and I'd rather not find out I'm twice as stupid as I thought. Why didn't I think of this before? I look out at Just Carol. She is busy talking to Cave Man. Maybe I could develop a sudden case of stomach flu. The trick is I have to get it quick between the rounds. Not with a math problem sitting in front of me. I don't want it to look like I really couldn't do the question.

Only I'm too late now as the answer lady's helper kid has just given me the fifth question. Shoot. I tap my pencil on the desk. I don't like lies that require a big performance. And besides that, this question is way hard. It's about a group of kids and how old they are if one is twice another's age and so on. It's tricky and I have to do it twice to make sure I have the right answer.

When the buzzer rings and the helper kids check the cards, Keegan and Madison and two other smart kids from my class are out. But I am not. I have my hand raised to tell the answer lady I've got to throw up, when one of the smart kids looks back at me. He is clearly surprised that I am up here and he is not. Something about this makes my blood burn, and when the answer lady calls on me, my mouth answers, "Never mind." But as soon as they hand out the seventh-round questions, I'm furious at myself. Why didn't I go when I had the chance? This one is way too hard. What if I really am stupid? I shouldn't try my hardest. This is a dumb idea. If I try my hardest and fail, then what?

My face feels sweaty. My armpits are hot. Now I hate Just Carol. It's her fault I'm going to make a fool of myself. Why did she come to this Math-a-thon, anyway? Art teachers aren't supposed to come to Math-a-thons. If she wasn't here, I'd leave right now. But while I'm thinking this, part of my brain is busy working the problem. My pencil is figuring the computations. They take a long time and that big second hand is ticking loud. *Ker-tick. Ker-tick. Ker-tick.*

I figure the answer with thirty seconds to spare and I breathe easier. I walk up to give my page to the answer lady, when suddenly I see the mistake. It pops up in my brain, like toast from the toaster. I sit down in a close-up seat and change the answer, then race to the answer lady just as the buzzer goes off.

The answer lady's head is down as she checks our answer cards. There are only three of us now, so she doesn't need help from the helper kids. I look over at Joyce Ann Jensen. She got her answer in early. She does her homework early, too. I wonder if she eats her breakfast the night before so she can have that done early, too.

The answer lady's head shoots up. She smoothes her blue dress. I don't want to hear what she says. But I am dying to know.

The PA clicks on. I keep looking at Harrison, pretending to ignore the answer lady. "Hmm, I can't read this," the answer lady says. "It must be Ann. Ann Mac-Fur-son," the answer lady says. "The District 2 Math Champion for the sixth grade is Miss Ann Mac-Fur-son from Sarah's Road School. Jasper Schwartz from Laredo Middle School and Joyce Ann Jensen from Sarah's Road School are our runners-up. Congratulations to all of you!"

Harrison hears, too. He pushes his hair out of his

eyes and smiles at me. Then he jumps on the stage and walks to the microphone.

The answer lady looks very uncomfortable, like he isn't supposed to be up there and maybe she should call the National Guard. I am wondering what the heck he's doing. This is very un-Harrison-like behavior.

"Excuse me," Harrison says. He takes the microphone. "Her name is Ant," he says. Then he hands the microphone back to the answer lady.

"Ant," the answer lady tries this out, "Ant Mac-Furson."

Harrison is smiling his one-dimpled smile. Apparently he's not so worried anymore. He actually looks proud, as if we won this together. And I guess in a way we did.

Everybody is clapping. Just Carol and Cave Man are cheering and stamping their feet. The answer lady gives me a big old trophy cup and a certificate for a free ice cream sundae from 31 Flavors, and some guy in a knit hat is taking my picture. I think about how there are no trophies this big in my house.

There is a big smile on my face. I don't mean for it to be there, it just is. It isn't a phony smile, either. It's like the feelings inside me are spilling out the hole in my face. I look out at the audience. There isn't one person in this whole auditorium who thinks I'm stupid. No one here thinks Elizabeth is smarter than me, either. No one cares about Elizabeth at all. Everyone is clapping for me! No wonder Elizabeth likes this so much.

Just Carol seems very excited. She can hardly stop talking about what happened. She insists I describe every single problem, even the easy ones. I do, except I leave out the part about the stomach flu I was planning to get and how if I hadn't seen her I would have walked out before the thing even started. I'm so happy I didn't do this.

When Just Carol is finally out of questions, she looks around, and I think she is wondering if my mother is here. Then she says, "I'd love to take you two to lunch. Would you like to call your parents and see if it's okay?"

"Sure," I say, mostly because I don't want this all to end. I want her to keep asking me questions and thinking I am smart for the whole rest of the day.

When I call, no one is at my house. I leave a message on the tape where I am, then Harrison and Just Carol and me go to lunch. We go to McDonald's and I have only French fries. Just Carol lets me, too. That is how great this day is.

When we get to my house, my mom is in the yard clipping dead lavender off a bush. Kate is sitting in the shade of our maple tree, rolling pennies. My mom looks up at the sound of Just Carol's car. She sets her clippers down, straightens her straw hat, and walks toward us. The trophy is so big, Just Carol put it in the trunk and now she has jumped out of the car to get it. She picks up my shiny brass trophy and hands it to me. The way she does this, it is as if I've won it all over again.

"So what is this?" my mother asks. She holds her chin with one hand and her elbow with the other. She stares at the trophy like she's never seen one before.

"Antonia won first place in the Math-a-thon," Just Carol explains. "We are all very proud of her." Just Carol is smiling so wide, the corners of her mouth are practically touching her dangly earrings.

"You know, I've always been good in math, too," my mother says. She smiles at Just Carol.

Just Carol nods. She stares at the trowel in my mom's pocket.

"And you were there in your capacity as an art teacher?" my mother asks.

Just Carol frowns. "More or less."

"I'm surprised they had room for you but not for any of the parents," my mother says.

"Room?" Just Carol asks.

My mother stares at me. "I thought you told me they couldn't get the gym space. They had to hold it in the library, so they uninvited all the parents." She waits for me to say something. I say nothing. I am swinging my trophy by one of its handles. I know I have to be careful here. I can't lie to Just Carol. That is our deal.

My mother runs her tongue over her teeth. "Apparently, that isn't true," my mother says.

"The Math-a-thon was in the auditorium. There was plenty of room," Just Carol says. She is looking at me. I wonder if she is going to be mad about this.

"Liar, liar, Ant's on fire," Kate sings from her patch of shade under the maple tree.

"Well, I couldn't have gone, anyway. It was my eldest daughter's dress rehearsal for *The Nutcracker*. She is Clara, you know," my mother says as she runs her hand down her neck. It is long like mine. Not squat like Your Highness's. I have never noticed this before.

"No, of course you couldn't," I say as I start toward the house. "Everybody understands that."

"What exactly do you mean by that, young lady?" my mother asks me.

"Nothing, I'm only agreeing with you is all. I am in complete agreement," I say as I pull open the front door.

20
FaMILY NIGHT aT CHEVY'S

It is Saturday night and my father is coming home from New York. We are picking him up at the airport and then he's taking us out to dinner at Chevy's. I love Chevy's, mostly because of those plain tortillas they have and the free refills on root beer, which come with maraschino cherries, if you ask.

My mother has already told us that my father doesn't know if he got the job or not. She says they are thinking about it and he won't know until next week. Still, Elizabeth and me aren't taking any chances. We are going to start working on him as soon as we see him.

When my dad gets in the car, Elizabeth begins right in kissing up to him. She is so good at this. She and my mom and dad are laughing now as if they are the only people in the world. I'm a little unhappy, but not as much as usual, because I know Elizabeth is on special assignment. She is working full-time to get on my dad's good side. We need her there.

When we get inside, Kate studies the menu to see how much everything costs. "If I order something cheaper than Elizabeth and Antonia, can I have the difference in cash?" Kate asks.

"I like your entrepreneurial spirit," my dad says. "But I don't think so, honey. Why don't you just order what you want to eat."

"Anything on the whole menu?"

My mother shakes her head no. "Anything on the kids' menu," she says.

We order and our dinner comes fast. I gobble down two plain tortillas because I'm really hungry. I am on my second root beer when my father says, "I have some good news."

Elizabeth and I look at each other. He wasn't supposed to have any news at all. We look at our mom. She is breaking bits of her tostada shell and making a little pile of fried tortilla pieces. I have never seen her do this.

"I'm not going to be working so hard anymore. I'm going to have a lot more free time for all of you." My dad smiles his big salesman smile.

"Did you get the job here?" Elizabeth asks. She is staring at my dad like she has X-ray eyes that can see through his brain. I'm afraid to look at him directly. I try to skewer the cherry in my root beer. Kate doesn't seem to understand what's happening. She is busy coloring the chili peppers on the kids' paper place mat.

"I got the job. I'm not going to be in charge of new offices. They'll be some travel, but not as much. And the lady I'm going to be working for is really terrific. It's a little more money and a lot more respect."

My mother is digging at her mashed-up corn with

the red cactus-shaped chip, which is supposed to be a garnish. If it were me doing this, she would tell me to stop playing with my food.

My dad's smile seems uneasy now. He is looking from my mom to Elizabeth to Kate to me.

Elizabeth begins her nervous rocking motion. Her hands are covering her face as if she doesn't want to see what will happen next.

"You said the job was here, right?" I tap on the table. I'm not looking at him. I can't bear for him to look me in the eye and tell me this isn't true.

"Where is the job?" Elizabeth asks.

"Now look, honey . . . ," my father says.

"Where?" Elizabeth repeats, louder and tougher this time.

My father sighs. "You can't just look at one isolated factor. You have to look at the big picture. You have to take a step back and consider . . ."

Elizabeth blows air through her nose and shakes her head. She closes her eyes. The tears squeeze through her closed lids. "Mom, is the car open? May I have the keys?" she asks.

"Elizabeth, let's talk about this," my father says. "It isn't that bad. I'm not taking you to some Godforsaken part of the country, you know. We're going to Connecticut. It's lovely there, truly it is. And—"

"Please, Mom, the keys." Elizabeth wiggles her outstretched hand. Her eyes are wet. She isn't looking at anyone.

My mother digs the keys out of her purse and drops them in Elizabeth's hand.

My father's eyes are confused. He really doesn't understand. "Connecticut is a beautiful place. You've never even been there. You don't know. We are about to get the things we want in our lives. The things your mother and I have worked so hard for . . ."

Elizabeth's chair squeaks against the floor as she pushes it back. She places the cord of her small pink purse on her shoulder, runs her hand through her hair, and walks across the floor. We all watch her go. Other people in the restaurant do, too.

"You know, she's the last person I expected to act this way," my father tells my mom. He looks in my eyes. For a second, he seems to think about pitching to me, then he settles on Kate. She is his fan club now.

"I work so hard for you—all of you . . . ," he tells Kate. "This is a really good move for me. Less travel. More money. I get out from under that lunatic Dave."

Kate is watching my father with complete attention. She is interested in the way he does everything.

"How much more money?" Kate asks.

"Well, more. Let's leave it at that." My father smiles. He loves this.

"Do they have Wells Fargo in Connecticut?" Kate asks.

"I'm not sure," my father says.

"Because I can't go if I have to change banks. When you have to change banks, there are fees. They told me that when I opened my account."

"I'm leaving," I say. "None of this really concerns me, anyway. I'm not a part of this family. I never have been." I look straight at my dad.

"Jesus Christ, Antonia, can't you think of a better game than that?" my mother says. She is holding her head, like it hurts.

I walk past the tortilla machine that is stamping air because no one has fed it any of those dough balls. I walk past the sombrero filled with peppermint candies. I walk out the door.

In the parking lot I find our blue Honda with my dad's suitcase in the back. Elizabeth is sitting in the backseat. Her face is buried in her hands. She is sobbing like I have never seen her cry before.

I don't say anything. I sit there watching a man load his groceries into the cab of his metallic green truck. I am angry—angry at myself. I should never have believed my dad. Never.

When we get home, Elizabeth goes straight to her room. I scoop up Pistachio, walk into the hall, and knock on Elizabeth's door. She has her Do Not Disturb, Dancer in Training sign on the door.

"Who is it?" she calls out.

"Me," I say.

"Enter," she says.

I open the door a crack and poke my head in. Elizabeth is sitting on her bed, needlepointing. She is working on a screen that has two pink satin ballet slippers painted on. The ribbons from the slippers spell the words "Strive for Excellence" in curvy pink handwriting. "Can I bring Pistachio in?" I ask.

"Just don't put him down," she says without looking up from her work. I stare at her room. It is so pink, it makes me feel as if I'm looking through pink-tinted glasses. When Elizabeth likes something, she likes it all the way.

"Think Mom will stop him?"

Elizabeth blows air out of her mouth. "Has she ever?"

"No. But I don't think she wants to move."

Elizabeth shrugs. "She's sick of rentals. She wants her own house."

"We need to do something," I say.

She shrugs again.

"Any ideas?" I ask.

Elizabeth shakes her head. She doesn't look up.

I look at Elizabeth. She is sad, but there is something else. Something fishy. It isn't like her to give up. "What's going on?" I ask.

She jerks the needle through the screen, but says nothing.

"Come on!"

She looks up at me. "If you tell Kate, I'll kill you," she says.

"Tell Kate what?"

"Promise on Pistachio's life. Touch him and say it, but don't let him down. I don't want him stinking up my room," Elizabeth commands.

I put my left hand on Pistachio's back and my right hand up in the air. "I promise on Pistachio's life," I say.

"I'm going to stay with Miss Marion Margo until after *The Nutcracker* and then maybe the next year. And then who knows, maybe I'll stay with her forever!"

"What about me?"

"You don't need to stay here the way I do."

"Yes, I do."

"Oh, please . . . because of Harrison? I'm sure there are people who smell like salami sandwiches in Connecticut, too. Maybe you'll even find someone better. Someone who smells like bologna."

"Shut up," I say.

"I'm sorry, but I have a career to consider," she says.

"A career?"

"I'm going to be a ballerina."

I groan and shake my head. "Your neck's too short."

"Shut up," she says.

"Shut up yourself," I say. I know I should leave now, but somehow I don't want to. I can't believe this. I can't believe she's serious. "When are you going to tell Mom?" I ask.

"I'm not going to. I'm going to have Miss Margo do it."

This makes me crazy, mostly because I see how clever it is. My mom will never say no to Miss Marion Margo. She thinks Miss Marion Margo is an utterly perfect human being. "It doesn't matter. I don't need you, anyway, because my real parents are coming any day now," I say.

"Oh, right. Just like Santa Claus and the Easter bunny," Elizabeth says.

"Fine." I shrug. "Don't believe me, then. But they are coming tomorrow morning at ten," I say. My heart is beating in my head. I am shaking, I am so angry. Even so, I know this is the stupidest thing in the world to say.

Elizabeth makes a rapid fire *hut-hut-hut* sound in the back of her throat. "That'll be the day."

"They are . . . so just shut your ugly face!" I storm out of her room and slam the door so hard her Dancer-in-Training sign falls off. I go to my room and blast my door, too. Then I put Pistachio on the bed. He is shaking and looking at me. He hates it when I get angry. It is the one thing in the world that terrifies him. I whisper to him and pet his wiry hair. When he is calmed down, I get out my real parents' book:

Dear Real Mom,

I don't get it. Why do we move so much more than other people? Why? It's not as if Dad works for the army or something. How come his jobs never last long? How come he gets a job and then decides it isn't THE ONE? Why are they always wrong? And how come my mom always goes along with it? How come she never says no? And why didn't my dad tell me the truth in the first place? Why did he lie about where the job was? That was lousy. It was.

Love,

Ant and Pistachio

P.S. I told Elizabeth you would be showing up tomorrow. I know you're not going to be there because you don't exactly exist to anyone but me. But Pistachio thinks maybe you will come. You know how he is.

21
MY REaL PaREnTS

I am sitting on the front steps of my house. My two books are in my lap. The one full of photos of me and artwork. The other with letters to my real parents. They are covered in a patchwork of rickrack, buttons, and lace.

I also have a backpack full of stuff: my orange jumper with all the zippers, my plaid pants, my Flintstones toothbrush, and my blown-glass deer babies. Plus I have food for Pistachio because he's supposed to have this special kind that's hard to find. And I have Pistachio's leash and a chew toy for him. He's asleep in a patch of sun over by the mailbox. He is like a lizard. He loves to sleep in the sun.

It is Sunday morning. My dad and my mom are sleeping late. Kate is watching TV and Elizabeth is in the kitchen. I want to say good-bye, because I want them all to know I am leaving. But I haven't yet.

I don't have a watch, so I go peek in the kitchen to see what time it is. It is ten minutes until ten o'clock. Your Highness is at the counter eating a bowl of Lucky Charms. She seems to have forgotten I said my real parents are coming this morning. I don't remind her. I don't want her hovering, waiting to make fun of me. Besides, I haven't exactly figured out what I'm doing. Maybe I'm running away.

"Have you even talked to Miss Marion Margo about going to live with her? Does she even know about this plan?" I ask.

Your Highness's head jerks up from her bowl. "Will you shut up about that? God, you have a big mouth!"

I shrug. "Kate's watching TV, she couldn't hear if I screamed in her ear," I say.

"She better not find out. You swore on Pistachio, and that's all I have to say." Your Highness shakes her cereal spoon at me.

"So, have you?" I whisper.

"Why do you care?"

"Just curious," I say, though I am more than curious. I can't stand that Elizabeth has figured out a way to stay and I haven't. It drives me nuts that she is even finding a new family better than me. I go back outside and sit on the steps. They are hard cement and my butt is tired of sitting here. It's so stupid that I am doing this. But I can't get myself to get up and go.

The lady across the street is planting flowers. She is wearing a floppy green hat that ties under her chin and stretch shorts. She waves at me. I wave back, though I hope she doesn't come over and ask a lot of questions. I don't feel like coming up with some big story to explain what I'm doing.

How long am I going to wait? If I'm going to leave, I should do it now. I pull my jacket out of my backpack and sit down on it. The step is a little softer this way.

The lady across the street goes inside. I'm glad she hasn't asked me what I'm doing, but I'm sorry she's gone inside, because now I have nothing to watch.

Now my dad comes out. He's carrying a couple of golf clubs, a tee, and two balls. He will probably practice his swing on the lawn. He doesn't get to go golfing very often, but he practices his swing a lot.

"It looks like you're at a bus stop there, Antonia," he says. He slips a golf ball in his pocket. "What are you doing?"

"Waiting."

"Waiting for what?"

"Nothing."

"Nothing? You've been waiting for the last hour for nothing?"

I nod. I'm surprised he knows I've been here that long. But I'm happy about it, too. I hate to be invisible.

My father sets a tee in the grass, places a ball on it, then practices hitting the ball without ever actually touching it. I wonder why he does this. If I were him, I'd want to give the ball a good whack. I'd want to see how far it would go.

Now he's putting down one club and picking up another. He goes back and forth between clubs, still not hitting the ball.

"Are you going to hit that thing or what?" I ask.

"Antonia," he says, looking over at me. He shakes his head and groans as if he's sick of me. "If this is some kind of running-away theatrics . . ." He waves the golf club at me.

"If I were running away, why would I be sitting here?" I ask. This is a good question. I haven't exactly figured this out myself.

He tips the metal end of his golf club against the ball and seems to try to forget I am here.

After a few minutes, he sighs and looks up at me. "You know, I came out here to hit a few balls and clear my head. I don't have the energy to deal with you right now, Antonia."

"Take vitamins."

"What?"

"Take vitamins, then you'll have more energy."

"Very funny." His eye tracks the ball.

I watch him as he taps the ball. Once, twice, three times until it settles in the little dirt hole he dug.

"Not bad, huh, Antonia," he says, then seems surprised to see me sitting with my bag of stuff on the front step of our house.

"I'm going to get your mother." He sets his club against the tree and begins to walk toward the house.

"Wait, Dad! No! Please wait," I call.

He stops. His shoulders move as if they have heard what I said. He turns around.

"Why do you take Mom's side all the time now?" I ask.

"It's pretty clear the problems are yours, Antonia. Not hers."

"Well, that's because you hear everything from her. Don't you ever want to know my side?"

His chin gets stiff. His shoulders tighten. He flips his hand at me as if I am onstage and he is introducing me. I hate the way he does this. But I don't want him to get Mom, so I keep talking.

"She doesn't treat me the same as Elizabeth and Kate. She doesn't. It's like she loves being their mother and she hates being mine. She'd be happier if I didn't live here. She would."

When I say this last my nose feels tight and prickly. I'm not crying, but tears seem to have backed up into my nose.

He shakes his head. "You know, Antonia, you get what you put out in life. Elizabeth and Kate don't give trouble, so they don't get trouble. You give your mom trouble, she gives you trouble. You stop giving her trouble, she'll stop giving you trouble. It isn't so complicated as you make it."

"What about the opposite? What about if she stops giving me trouble, I'll stop giving her trouble. What about if she loved me, I'd love her. Why do you assume the problem starts with me?"

"Look, Antonia, I don't want to debate which came first, the chicken or the egg."

"How come everything I think is too much trouble for you to talk about?"

"I *am* talking about it."

"You just said you didn't want to have this discussion with me."

"What do you want from me, Antonia?"

I think about this. "Remember that time you took just me and Kate camping, and then in the middle of the night you saw a spider and got really scared and I had to hold your hand, and then we got to go to the

Holiday Inn and eat French toast with boysenberry syrup?"

"Yeah." He smiles a little. Not the smooth, charming smile. The funny smile I love.

"That was fun. When can we do that again? You're always working now. It's like you only have energy for me if I do exactly what you want. You only have space for a perfect daughter. You don't have room for me."

"Antonia, I do the best I can."

"Why do we have to move again, Dad? Why don't you get a new job here?"

My father makes a short angry noise, part groan, part grunt. "Antonia, I've been through this a hundred times with Elizabeth already. I'm not talking about the move anymore. I'm just not."

He heads toward the house. The door bangs shut behind him.

Inside, I hear him call my mother. My mother says something, but I don't hear what it is. "I tried to ignore her," my father says. I strain to make out the rest. I can't, but from the tone of it I know my father is telling on me. His voice sounds just like Kate or Elizabeth when they report to my mom about me.

Now my mother appears. She is dressed, but she hasn't fixed her hair or put on her makeup. She doesn't usually go outside looking this way. Not even to the front yard.

"What in the world are you doing, Antonia?" she asks.

"I'm waiting."

"Yes, I can see that, but what for?"

"Nothing."

"You don't go to the zoo today, do you?"

"No."

"Are you waiting for *that* teacher?" My mother always calls Just Carol "*that* teacher."

"No." I try as hard as I can not to cry. But I lose the battle. The tears spill down my face.

"Well, who are you waiting for?" I can see my mother is getting exasperated. But she seems alarmed, too. I almost never cry in front of her.

My lips form the words "My real mom," but I don't say them. I can't say them out loud. Instead I say, "You're not my real mom."

"Jesus, Mary, and Joseph . . . Antonia," my mother says.

"You're not," I say. My voice is hoarse and so full of tears I can hardly speak. "You don't love me. Neither does Daddy," I whisper.

My mother is frowning. Her lips get small and closed, like when you tie off a paper bag with a rubber band. "Don't be ridiculous!"

"You don't," I say.

"I don't cook what you like for dinner, I make you clean up your room, I punish you for getting bad grades, and what do you know." She snaps her fingers. "I'm not your real mother. You know, I'm really tired of it. I learned a long time ago that being a mother is not about winning a popularity contest. So

I don't expect you to say thank you for all the things I do for you. But I am up to here"—she puts her hand to her forehead— "with this nonsense."

I have heard this popularity contest speech a hundred times before. I know she will go inside now and leave me out here to "learn my lesson."

She sits down on the step. This surprises me. I move away from her, but I don't stop crying. I can't. The tears are pouring out of me.

She is quiet. Any moment I expect her to get up and go inside. But she doesn't.

"Antonia," she starts, but then she sighs and says nothing. We sit watching a hummingbird buzz around a blue flower and then fly off. I wish he would stay.

"Antonia," she tries again, "I do love you. I just don't understand you. And when I talk to you, I feel as if I'm talking to a brick wall. Like nothing I say gets through." She looks over at me. I can't stand to look at her. I focus on the speckled gray cement step. There is a slight glitter to it I never noticed before.

She sighs. "I get so frustrated with you, I could scream. And then I never know if you're telling the truth or not. I always feel like you're trying to make me look foolish."

"I don't want you to be my mother," I say, scooting as far away from her as I can while still sitting on the step.

"Well, some days I don't want you to be my daughter, either. But you are my daughter and I am your mother. We're stuck with each other, so maybe we should try to make the best of it. Now why don't you go and get yourself cleaned up and put that stuff away." She's tired of talking to me. Her voice has that I've-had-enough-of-this edge.

I don't move.

"What is that you're holding, anyway?" she asks.

"Books."

"Scrapbooks?"

"Sort of."

"They're pretty the way you've decorated them. Can I see?"

"They're for my real parents," I say.

"Antonia, you're way too old to make up stories like this. You don't really believe any of this, do you?"

She waits for me to answer. I say nothing.

"Do you?"

"Maybe," I say.

"May I look?" she asks, running her fingers over the cover of the book.

I shake my head so hard my hair flies in my face. "No." This is the only power I have. If I say yes, she will look at my books and tell me how silly I am for writing them. But if I tell her no, she'll always wonder. She'll never know what's inside.

She nods as if she's expecting this.

"Are you ready to come back inside?" she asks.

"No," I tell her, but I am.

After she leaves, I take my books, my backpack, and Tashi and I climb the back trellis and shimmy in through the hall window. Then I tiptoe back in my room. I don't want her to see me come back in. I have to win at least this much. I just do.

22
MY MOM'S PLAN

It is half past seven on Saturday and no one in my house is up except me. I like being awake when nobody else is. It makes me feel as if I have important things to do and all they have to do is sleep.

Besides, getting up early is a good way to avoid everybody, which I have been doing a lot lately. I'm pretending I'm a boarder in this house and I have no connection with anyone. I hate them all, anyway. I do. Pistachio is the only one who is totally on my side.

I look outside to see if Just Carol is here yet, but there are only parked cars on the street, the same ones that are here every morning and every night. I put my green plastic bowl in the dishwasher and get out my lunch so I will be ready when they come. I set my lunch sack on the desk by the door. Usually, my mom has everything neat on this desk. Bills, school flyers, coupons, everything has its own little cubby. But today, there are loose papers all over: moving estimates, notes about a security deposit, a Connecticut newspaper. And then I see a flash of purple. The color stops me. I know that purple. I have trained my eye to look for it so I can put it in the bottom of my bucket and cover it with dog poop. But wait, I tell myself. Just because a paper is purple doesn't mean it's one of those creepy pamphlets. It could be a flyer advertising a sale on vacuum cleaners. It could be anything. I tug the tiny corner of purple and pull the paper out. My chest tightens. The golden retriever is looking at me with his sad old eyes. The clock asks: "Is it time to euthanize?"

My eyes search out Pistachio. He is under my kitchen stool, curled in a ball, his nose resting on his tail. I try to think about when my mother could have gotten that brochure. And why? Maybe she needed a piece of scratch paper one day. I look to see if there is anything marked on it. There is. She circled something. "Changes in environment can be especially upsetting for an old animal. Plane flights, extended kennel stays, and long car trips are not advised."

I know my mom doesn't like to take Pistachio in the car. She says he sheds on the seats and makes the car smell like a kennel. My dad says we are going to rent a U-Haul truck and drive our stuff to Connecticut. But what about Pistachio? He can't go in the truck, and if my mom won't take him in her car . . .

And then it hits me. My mom's not planning to take him with us. She's planning to . . . My heart is beating fast. There is no way I am ever going to let Pistachio out of my sight. I will never leave him alone with my mother. Not ever. I scoop him up and go upstairs and get a book bag and slip him inside. Just Carol won't suspect the bag, because she'll think I have my lunch in it. I can't put my lunch in the bag with Pistachio, though, because he'll eat it. But I'll have to bring a sandwich, otherwise Just Carol will be suspicious. It won't make sense that I have brought a lunch bag and forgotten the food. I get some masking tape out of the drawer and I use practically the whole roll taping my sandwich and my banana to my belly. It's lucky I'm skinny and don't wear tight clothes. There is plenty of room to rebutton my jeans around the sandwich bag.

I'm stuffing my granola bar in my pocket when I see Just Carol's car in front of my house. I grab the bag with Pistachio in it and run outside. I am careful not to let the bag bounce against my legs as I run. I smile and look straight into Just Carol's eyes. "Hi," I say.

"Hi yourself." She smiles. Her hair is in a ponytail held with an orange scrunchie and she is wearing her brown Zoo Volunteer T-shirt.

I get in the car and place Pistachio's bag on the floor next to my feet.

"Where's Harrison?" I ask, hoping, praying Just Carol will say we're going to pick him up second today.

"He's got the flu."

"Oh," I say, so disappointed I can barely speak. How could he get sick today?

"He must be feeling pretty lousy to skip seeing Kigali," Just Carol says.

All I can think about is Pistachio in my bag. If he makes one noise, I'm dead. I look at Just Carol. I wonder if there's any chance we'll get lost on the way to the zoo and never get there. I keep hoping this the whole way until we pull into the zoo parking lot.

Just Carol stops the car and I pick up the bag with Pistachio in it and grab the cool metal door handle. My arm is resting on the toast-colored leather door. Slowly, I get out, but I don't let go of the door. When Just Carol pushes the master lock switch, I spring to action, shoving back inside the car before it's too late.

Pistachio and I are safely inside the car now. Just Carol is outside. I didn't plan to do this, I just did it. But now I feel better. No one can make me leave this car. Pistachio and I will stay in Just Carol's car for the rest of our lives. We will be safe here.

Just Carol taps on the side window. "Hey, Ant, what're you doing?"

I stare out the front window, my whole body stiff.

"Ant?"

I don't look at her.

"Ant? What are you doing?"

I say nothing. I look straight ahead out the windshield, as if I were driving the car and it would be dangerous to look in any other direction. Just Carol opens the driver-side door and climbs back in the car. *Fruuup*, the door closes. We sit quietly for a minute and then she whispers, "You want me to take you home?"

I shake my head. Just Carol sighs. I don't know what she is thinking because I don't look at her. I keep looking through the windshield. I try to make myself turn and look straight into her eyes because I know this is the only way to lie, but I can't.

"What's going on, Ant?"

I watch the branches of a big pine tree. There is just enough wind to make them do a little dance. Trees are so lucky. No one can make them move. They spend their whole lives in the same spot.

I open my mouth to say something. Nothing comes out. I try again. My voice sounds funny, like a tape recording of myself. "I've got Pistachio with me," I say.

Just Carol's teeth grind. I think about crying, but I'm afraid once I start, I won't stop.

"Why?" Just Carol asks.

I can't tell if she's mad or not and I am too upset to look at her. I take the purple pamphlet out of my pocket and hand it to her. "My mom had this. I'm afraid she wants to . . . I'm afraid . . ." My hand finds Pistachio's little body and I pull him out of the bag and bury my face in his scruffy fur. I smell his dirty ripe smell.

"Oh," Just Carol says. She is very quiet. I wonder if she is going to drive me home and never have anything to do with me again.

Just Carol sits for a moment, then she reaches over and squeezes my arm. "I'm proud of you, Ant. You told me the truth."

I feel relief ease my stiff neck, tense back, strained arms. She heard. She understood. I can't stop the tears now. They pour down my cheeks.

"Okay, this is what we're going to do. I'm going to borrow a rope and a dish. Then I'll fill the dish with water and bring it here. I'll pull the car up by those pine trees. We'll tie Pistachio outside the car with a dish of water. He'll be fine for a few hours. And as for your mom and Pistachio . . . we'll work that out. We will."

I like the sound of this. I like the "we" as if she is in this together with me. I wonder now if I should tell her about the move. But I don't want to. Something tells me that this is not a problem Just Carol can solve. My mouth stays closed. I sit quietly petting Pistachio while Just Carol is gone.

When she comes back, we get Pistachio set up. I'm not crazy about tying him here. I worry he will pull out of his collar or get twisted in the rope. But Just Carol is probably right. He'll be fine. I cinch Pistachio's collar up a notch so he can't possibly slip through, just to be sure.

Pistachio whines and jumps up and down all crazy when we leave, but this is for show. When we get far enough away, he makes a nest for himself on top of my book bag, curls up, and goes to sleep.

Just Carol keeps saying not to worry, we'll work it out, we'll figure out a plan, but first we need to report for work, otherwise Mary-Judy will have our hides.

Mary-Judy seems the least of my worries, but I follow along, glad to have someone tell me what to do, because my head is mush. We walk through the zoo entrance, by the flamingos, past the chimp with his teddy, and down to the bamboo fence with its Do Not Enter sign. As usual, all the khaki people are milling around down there. It's almost as if this is their cage at the zoo . . . the keeper exhibit.

Just Carol says hello to a skinny khaki person. We go into the room that smells like a pet store and pull on our boots, just like we always do, and march back out to follow Mary-Judy.

Mary-Judy says she's going to split us up. Just Carol is going to start cleaning the camel exhibit and I am going to help Mary-Judy with the aviary. Normally, I would be very excited about this because this means I get to feed the macaws. But today I want to stay close to Just Carol. Only when Mary-Judy says to do something, you do it. No questions asked. Besides, it's kind of an honor getting to go with Mary-Judy without Just Carol around. It means she trusts me. I like the feel of that. I like the feel of the extra set of keys she hands me, too. I hook them on my belt loop, the way Just Carol does.

Mary-Judy has fifty-seven animals to take care of, if you count the roans, the bison, and the python. There are only three keys, though. All the keepers carry three keys and a radio. The radio is important because the zoo is so big and being a keeper isn't the safest job in the world. Mary-Judy says Dora, the giraffe keeper, got pinned by a zebra once, and if it wasn't for her radio, she'd have been a goner. And then another time, a lion climbed the fence when there was a third-grade class right there. Mary-Judy says that was a long time ago. She says the only thing that happens now is a kid will drop his backpack from the aerial ride that goes over the lions' area, and then the next day when Mary-Judy walks the exhibit, she'll find a pink Barbie backpack torn to shreds. Of course, she doesn't know about how Pistachio was almost a Dog McNugget one day. Just Carol never told her about that.

While we work, we listen to the radio calls. Somebody's got a shipment of Pretty Bird. Where should it go? Pauline wants to know who took the hillside barn hay hooks and when maintenance is going to fix the snake windows. But today I am not paying much attention. I knock yesterday's fruit off the macaws' tree and worry about what I'm going to do when it's time to go home.

Soon we are done with the macaws and we head to the tiger exhibit. Mary-Judy turns on the hose. She pokes it through the chain link. The tiger has his own water dish, but he likes the hose water better. He is bony and old, and he has big kind eyes that are always asking a question. He is never scary, the way the lions are. I watch as he curls his tongue around the stream of water.

Mary-Judy turns the plastic Beware: Keeper in Exhibit Area sign over so everyone will know not to let the tiger out of his night house into the exhibit. Then she lets me open the exhibit with my own key. I am very excited about this. I've never had the keys to the cages before. I stick the key in the lock, then I look around to see if there is anyone to see me doing this.

When we get inside, Mary-Judy's radio begins to hum and get all staticky, the way it does when someone is about to talk. Then a voice says: "Come in all departments. Does anyone know anything about a little brown dog? Looks like maybe he was tied up somewhere. He's dragging one of our ropes. He's up here at the African exhibit, scaring my hoof stock out of their minds."

At first, I don't register what's been said. And then my mind replays the words: *Little brown dog . . . dragging one of our ropes.* I drop my bucket and race out of the tiger exhibit. I'm moving fast, but I'm intensely aware of everything. I see the fence, a crack in the pavement, a bucket we left outside. I feel the smack of pavement beneath my feet, the eucalyptus leaves brush my arm, the adhesive tape pulls at my stomach.

"Hey!" Mary-Judy screams, but there is no time to answer. No time to explain. I'm moving as fast as I can, uphill. My legs pull hard against the grade. I hear the thunder of hooves as I reach the crest of the hill. The gazelles are galloping, their delicate, spindly legs flying, hooves barely grazing the ground. The giraffes are running crazy. They seem scared and confused as they try to turn on their big long legs. A crane scurries out of the way. A frantic duck tries to fly, but his wings are clipped.

God, please don't let it be Pistachio and if it is him don't let him be inside. My feet are pounding the ground. This couldn't be happening, my mind says.

Dora, the giraffe keeper, is there. "WALK!" she screams. I don't know if she is talking to the animals or me.

"The little dog. Is the little dog here?" I cry, my voice breaking because I am out of breath.

"If one of my hoof stock breaks a leg because of your DAMN DOG . . ." Her face is big and red and angry.

"Where is he?" I scream.

"Over there." She points toward the elephant exhibit. "WALK, FOR GOD'S SAKE!" she screams, and then I know she's talking to me, but I don't walk. I can't.

"Pistachio!" I scream as I run toward the elephants.

23
THE KEY

When I get to the elephants, I'm so out of breath,
I'm doubled over. My throat feels like a Brillo pad and
I have a terrible side ache. I stop. It's hot and quiet.
The elephants are lazy. One is running his trunk along
the ground as if he's vacuuming. Another is itching
his butt on a big log. A third is sleeping in the shade of
a big oak tree. They are peaceful, slow moving, bored.
It looks like it would take a lot more than a tiny barking dog to get them upset. For a second, I am relieved.

I run past the exhibit to the elephant information
kiosk. I look behind it. Where is he? I look all around.
I wish he wasn't the color of dirt and so darn small.
There is a breeze blowing the big trees just outside the
exhibit. A mom pushes a stroller by me. "No, you can't
have any more fruit rolls. That's enough for today,"
she says.

"Pistachio," I cry. "Pistachio!" Though I sound frantic, the elephants don't even turn their heads.

"Which one is Pistachio?" the mom asks.

I'm running now. My big boots slap the pavement.
Something inside me says Pistachio isn't here. I re-

member how proud he was the day he scooted under the lions' fence. Utterly, completely, stupidly proud. I am running up the path around the back way to the lion exhibit—to the spot where Pistachio scooted under the fence before.

Mary-Judy is in the zoo truck speeding toward the elephants on the road below. She doesn't see me and I don't flag her down. I don't want to stop. I don't want to take the time. I don't want her with me, because if Pistachio is in the lion exhibit, I know Mary-Judy won't let me get him out.

By the time I pass the zebra-striped bathroom, my chest is killing me, and the masking tape, which is holding my sandwich to my belly, is pulling like crazy. I jump over the fake wood fence and cut down to the back of the lion exhibit. The lions are up the hill near a big ball that hangs from a tree with a thick chain. They aren't playing with the ball. They are all four sleeping, lazy in the tall brown grass.

"Pistachio!" I call, forcing myself to sound calm. I don't want the lions to know I'm upset. I'm afraid to tell them Pistachio is here. I'm afraid they might understand my words, even though this doesn't make sense.

"Pistachio!" I call again, looking around. Usually, he comes when he's called. Usually he can't wait to see me. The only time he won't come is if he gets so interested in something, he just can't turn away.

"Pistachio!"

I hear something. A sharp cry around by the side. I follow the fence toward the sound. And then, all of a sudden, I see him. He is in the exhibit dancing on his hind legs. He does a little jig when he hears my voice, but he doesn't come to me. He can't. His rope is wound around a bush. It's caught. He can't move. He's a sitting duck for those lions. Lunch, delivered to their door. Once they see him, he is dead. "Oh, Pistachio," I whisper, my pulse booming in my ears.

I look up at the fence, thinking I will climb over, and then I realize *I have the keys*. I feel happy about this and terrified at the same time. I almost wish I didn't have them. My hand goes to my belt loop. The keys jangle against my fingers. I unclip them. My heart is beating so loud, I can't hear anything else. I am so scared my hands fumble. Which key?

First one doesn't turn. I shove the second key in. The padlock falls open in my hand. I unchain the entrance and slip inside, half closing the gate behind me.

Then I stop, my hand gripping a chain-link diamond. Pistachio is straining against the rope, trying as hard as he can to get to me. My hand eases its grip on the fence. Then, my fingers let go and I move toward him. I remember Mary-Judy saying that sudden motion will catch a lion's eye, but I have to get to Pistachio. There is no way to do that without moving.

Don't look at the lions, I tell myself. Don't. But I have to. One is standing. Her whole body taut. Waiting. Watching. Daring me to move. "Be tall," Just Carol told me once when I was helping her feed the bison on the hill. If they come close, tell them to leave, and be tall. I pretend I am the tallest person in the world. I walk in slow, smooth, gliding steps. I take a quick, reckless look at the lions. Four sets of big glinting gold eyes are tracking me. One lion is standing. I half rush, half glide. The closer I get to Pistachio, the more he crazy jumps. "Stop it," I whisper, "stop doing that." But he pays no attention.

I'm running now. My boots are moving almost without my consent. I tear fast clear out of one rubber boot to Pistachio and yank the rope, but it's too twisted around the bush. It will take too long to untangle. I grab at Pistachio's collar. Untie the rope from his collar? Unbuckle the collar from his neck? My fingers are dumb as sticks. Won't go. Won't move. I hear her. I see a blur of gold fur coming for me. My stupid fingers work the buckle. The collar falls free. Pistachio is mine. I clutch him against my belly as I run, my legs moving, my feet flying. One sock. One boot. I can hear the lion behind me now. She is behind me. *Behind me.* I run faster. Pain in my sock foot. Get to the gate. To the gate. To the gate. My fingers curl around the chain link. I swing the gate open and I am out.

24
MaRY-JuDY

I am sitting in the dirt outside the lion exhibit, holding Pistachio tight. I can feel his little heart beating. I can feel my own beating, too. I can't believe we are both safe. I pet him and pet him and pet him. I can't get enough of petting him.

Inside the fence, the lioness finds Pistachio's collar. She is chewing and licking it. Chewing and licking. A chill goes up my spine. I can't watch.

Mary-Judy is here. I'm not sure when she got here, but she seems to know exactly what happened. She doesn't yell at me. She asks me if I am okay—whispers it. From the look on her face, I think it would be better if she'd yelled.

Now, she is pacing back and forth, talking into her radio. *Fook, fook, fook* goes her big rubber boots. "Come in, Dora? What's the status at the African exhibit? You need help?" *Fook, fook, fook.* She paces. Her radio crackles. The voice comes through loud and clear. "The gazelles are still jumpy as hell, but they aren't running themselves crazy anymore. I think I'm better off handling them myself. New people will only get them riled up again."

"Okay," Mary-Judy says. *Fook, fook, fook.* She checks the chain on the lion exhibit. Her hands are shaking. She has checked the lock three times already. I wonder if she thinks I got in because she forgot to lock it. But this can't be true, because she has taken the keys back from me. She did this first thing, her hands shaking. *Fook, fook, fook.* She stops in front of me. "Get in the truck," she commands. She is still whispering. I don't know why.

I stand up, holding Pistachio tight against my belly. I get in the truck. The truck is still running. The keys are dangling from the ignition. Mary-Judy must have jumped out so fast, she didn't take the time to turn it off. The armrest is missing from my door, so there's nothing to pull to close it. I roll down the window and grab hold of the frame. I slam twice before it shuts.

Mary-Judy scoots her bottom onto the seat. She is so short, she has to sit on a pillow to see over the dashboard. She puts the truck in gear and gives the accelerator a little punch. My neck jerks as the truck jolts forward down the hill. She's not looking at me. Not talking to me. I wonder where she is taking me.

Mary-Judy pulls the truck out to the road by the camel exhibits. She slows to let a cluster of kids move out of the way. When they are safely gathered on the side of the road, she creeps the truck forward to the camels' night house, then stomps on the brakes. The brakes squeak. The truck stops. Mary-Judy jumps out. "Stay here. Do not move! *Do not move!*" she whispers in a hoarse voice, and then seems to think better of leaving me in the truck with the keys in the ignition. She swings back in, turns off the motor, and pockets the keys.

Mary-Judy fast walks into the camels' night house, a low brown building that is strangely round, like a giant mushroom head. A few minutes pass and then *fook, fook, fook,* she is back with Just Carol in tow. When I see Just Carol, I look down. I study the floor of the truck. It is muddy and corroded, completely worn in places, so I can see through to the road below. I inspect every square inch of the floor and what I can see of the road. The truck door opens, and I automatically scoot over to make room for Just Carol, but I do not look at her.

"Are you okay?" Just Carol asks me. She stares at my one sock foot. It is sore. I stepped wrong on a rock. But I am okay.

I nod, wishing I could say no, because if I was hurt, she wouldn't be so mad at me. I hate having her mad. But what was I supposed to do? Let the lions eat Pistachio? It wasn't my fault, I feel like screaming. But I sit quiet, inspecting the toe of my sock. I hate people. They are too complicated. Dogs are way better. Dogs never chew you out or get disappointed in you. They understand everything. They are loyal, no matter what.

Mary-Judy drives us down the road to the Do Not Enter sign. She gets out of her truck and opens the gate. This is a job Just Carol usually does. That Mary-

Judy hasn't let her is a bad sign. Mary-Judy gets back in and pulls the truck up to the building where our lockers are. "Get your stuff. I'll wait!" Mary-Judy whispers.

Just Carol and I get out. There is another keeper sitting at the picnic table. She is staring at us like we are criminals. I take off my boot and stuff my feet in my sneakers without untying. Just Carol gets her lunch out of the refrigerator. Mine is still taped to my belly, which is uncomfortable, and I know it's going to hurt like heck to pull off.

We climb back in the truck and I wonder where we are going. Then I get it. We are being thrown out, Just Carol and me. Oh, great! This wasn't Just Carol's fault, it was an accident. Nobody meant for Pistachio to come untied. I think about trying to explain this to Mary-Judy. I look over at her hard, scared face and I decide against it. She's not going to change her mind about this right now.

Mary-Judy drives us out to the parking lot. She drives up to Just Carol's car and stops so close, I can hardly squeeze out. Still, Mary-Judy doesn't say anything. Not one word. She waits while Carol unlocks the car, gets in, puts on her seat belt. She waits while Just Carol starts the car. She is still waiting when we drive out of the parking lot.

I feel tired and shaky. My head is buzzing and I'm worried about Pistachio, who is burrowing into me like he is scared. I have been petting him so much, my hand feels numb to the feel of his fur. I look over at Just Carol and wonder what she is thinking as she drives down the long zoo road. She is so quiet, I can't tell.

We are driving through the grass hills, green from a recent rain. I look again at Just Carol. Her face is blank. I can't read her, but it's bad that she's so quiet.

"I didn't lie," I blurt out. "I had to go in there, otherwise Pistachio would have . . . otherwise the lions would have . . ."

"Do you have any idea how lucky you are?" Just Carol interrupts. "Mary Judy said she can't figure out why the lions didn't get you. She said she'd never have believed you could have gotten out of there in one piece."

"I couldn't just leave him!"

"Why didn't you ask for help?"

"How do I know Mary-Judy would have helped? How do I know she wouldn't have just left him in there?"

"You're always a one-man show, aren't you, Ant? You're your own country. But I guess what really upsets me is how you consistently value Pistachio's life over your own."

I shake my head and stare at the gas station we are driving by. Just Carol is really stepping on the gas pedal. I wish she would slow down. I don't want to get home so fast.

"It's true," Just Carol says. "On the other hand, I do feel partly to blame. It was my idea to tie up Pistachio."

I glance over at her. Her eyes are drilling into me. She is looking at me so long, I worry she will drive off the road. "My dog was in trouble, so I helped him. Anybody in the world would have done the same as me."

"You think so?"

"Any kid would've. Nobody would let their dog die. Even Joyce Ann Jensen would break a rule to save her dog."

Just Carol shakes her head like she can't believe me. "You just don't get it, do you, Ant? It isn't about breaking rules. It's about your life."

"I'm fine," I say. "I didn't get hurt."

She says nothing. I hate when she goes quiet like this. We are getting close to my house. I'm afraid she's not going to say anything else, so I start again. "I am sorry about you losing your zoo job. Really I am."

"Yeah . . . me, too."

"Any chance you can get it back . . . you know, after Mary-Judy cools off?"

She shrugs. "I don't know, Ant. I'm too upset now to think about it."

Oh no! What about Harrison? What if he can't go to the zoo anymore, either? I can't believe what a mess this is.

"So, what now?" I ask.

"What now? Now I'm going to take you home." Just Carol reaches for her sunglasses.

"You said we'd work out, you know, the problem I told you about before." I know I shouldn't say this. Not now. But I can't help it. I don't know what else to do.

She sighs. "Look, I'll talk to your mom about her

plans for Pistachio, but before I do that, you need to talk to her."

"*Me?*"

"Yes."

"That's impossible."

"No, it's not. I shouldn't be in the middle of this. You need to talk to her."

We are almost at my house now. This is my only chance. "How about if I talk to you, instead of her. We could talk . . . all the time. You know, me and you. And you could take care of me—not that I need a lot of taking care of. I'm practically grown up and I take care of myself."

I can't believe I've said this. My stomach drops down, the way it does when the elevator goes down too fast. I feel woozy. My head is hot. My ears are hot, too. I wish I could crawl under the seat.

I can feel Just Carol looking at me.

"I'm just kidding," I whisper, my voice suddenly hoarse. "That was only a joke."

We are at my house now. Just Carol pulls up in front of the cement path, turns off the key, crosses her arms. "What's going on, Ant?"

I stare out the window, unable to say more. Just Carol is quiet, too. We watch the neighbor's yellow Volkswagen pull into the garage.

"Ant?"

All I can think about is going upstairs to my room, barricading the door with the dresser, and getting under the covers with Pistachio.

"Ant?"

"The MacPhersons are moving again. To Connecticut," I whisper.

"Oh," Just Carol says. It is long the way she says it. More like a sound than a word.

25
ELIZaBETH

I am standing outside my house. Just Carol is gone. She has been gone for several minutes now, but I haven't moved. I'm too upset to move. It's not that she said no, because she didn't. She didn't say yes, either. "I don't really know if that would be the best thing for you, Ant" were Just Carol's exact words. Hah. I know that line. It really means "I don't know if that would be the best thing for *me*." I love how grown-ups pretend they are looking out for you, when they are really looking out for themselves.

Still, I haven't given up hope. But I'm not exactly going to wait around for Just Carol to make up her mind, either. I'll peel my lunch off my belly, get my stuff, and go to Harrison's house. I know this is a dumb plan. If I'm gone, the first place my mom will look is Harrison's house. And Mr. Emerson will make me call my mom, anyway. He'll never let me run away there. But this is the only idea I have right now. I tell my feet to walk forward. Both my mom's car and my dad's car are gone, so at least I'll have the house to myself.

My feet walk across the lawn to the side door and my hands try the knob. It is open. Then I see why. Elizabeth is in the kitchen. She is sitting on the counter, swinging her legs. "Hey," she says in her perky voice. "Boy, am I glad to see you!"

I look around to see if someone is behind me.

"*You*, dummy," she says.

"Why are you glad to see me?" I ask as I get Pistachio a drink of water. After what he's been through, he's probably really thirsty.

"Because I need your help. Look, you got the edge with Mom right now. You know what she told me yesterday? She said you 'turned over a new leaf.' "

"I did not."

"I guess she went to get a copy of your report card because you didn't bring home the right one, which is *so weird*." She shakes her head. "She said you got mostly A's."

"I DID NOT TURN OVER A NEW LEAF!" I scream.

"Fine, fine, you're the same dirty old leaf side. Geez." She shakes her head and juts her chin out. "Do you want to hear my idea or not?"

I roll my eyes. Elizabeth takes my hand and pulls me into the living room. She points at the couch, where I am supposed to sit down. This is just like Elizabeth. She can't have a regular conversation. Everything is a performance.

"Okay," Elizabeth says. She is standing in front of me with one finger in the air, her whole body tense, as if she is waiting for the music to begin. "You talk to

Mom about how happy you are now and how you don't know if you can move, because it's been such a struggle for you—turning over a new leaf—" She mouths this part and then jumps all the way around to demonstrate. "You are doing better in school now *and* you have friends—but don't mention Harrison, she hates him. That art teacher lady. Talk about her—*and* you think the move to Connecticut would be too much for you *and* you'd go back to your old ways *and* probably end up in juvenile hall. But don't make it a threat or anything!"

I groan and bury my face in my hands.

"And I'm going to work on the golf thing with Dad. In Connecticut you can't play golf year round, you know. So even if he has more time, what's he going to do with it? And you'll work the human suffering angle with Mom. You're fragile." She grabs a glass pear from on top of the TV, then leaps around the room with it. "You could go bad in Connecticut. And then Mom will have to go on one of those talk shows and explain how she let her daughter turn into a delinquent. And she's going to have to figure out what to wear when she has to sit in court because you're on trial for things, like murder and stuff."

I snort and roll my eyes.

"And if you really turn out bad, they'll cover it on TV, and then everybody will see what a bad mother she is. That's a good angle." Elizabeth points at me. "You should mention that."

"In the first place, it's not going to work. And in the second place, what's it to you, anyway? I thought you were going to live with Miss Marion Margo?" I walk back into the kitchen to get the scissors. Pistachio follows along behind me. I get the good scissors and hold my T-shirt up with my teeth. I try to work the blade into the gap between the banana and the tape.

"Of course it will work." Elizabeth leaps into the kitchen. "What are you doing? Why did you tape a banana to your belly? God, you are so weird."

"I had to take Pistachio in my lunch bag. There wasn't room for my lunch," I say. Pistachio seems better now. He is wiggling his little body and doing a dance by the shelf where I keep his Milk-Bones. I am glad to see this. I can't quite believe that just an hour ago, he was inside the lions' cage. I think about telling Elizabeth this, but I decide against it. Elizabeth isn't going to listen right now. Her head is full of plans. Besides, there's no way she'll believe me.

"Why did you put him in your lunch bag? Do you know how gross that is? He probably shedded in there. Did you take your thermos, too? Because if you did, you're going to have dog hair in your milk for the rest of the year."

I'm not really paying attention to her because I'm concentrating on getting one-half of the scissors blade worked up under the adhesive tape. I wish I'd thought about how hard this would be to get off before I put it on. I didn't need to put on this much tape.

"Here, let me do that," she says. I hand her the scissors. Normally I wouldn't do this, but Elizabeth is good with her hands. If anyone can get this tape off without taking half my skin with it, it is Elizabeth.

o into the bathroom and she makes me take
t off. Then she walks all the way around me as
s planning her attack. I feel funny standing in
my bra with the cups that wrinkle over because I don't
exactly fill them out the way you're supposed to. I
hope Elizabeth doesn't say anything about this. Her
breasts aren't any bigger than mine, but she spends
two hours in the dressing room at Penney's until she
finds a bra that fits perfect. I can't be bothered with
this.

"I think it's better if we do a fast pull," she says.
"It's going to hurt more, but it will be over quicker."

I nod. "Just tell me when."

"When." She takes the tape and rips it off.

"OUCH!" I scream. It feels as if she's ripped my
flesh off.

"Hold still," she says, and rips again.

"Ouch!" I yell again.

"Almost done," she says just the way our mother
does. "One more."

"Ouch!" I scream again.

"That's it." She hands me the scissors. She is smiling like what would the world do without her.

"Thanks," I mumble. "But don't change the subject. What happened with Miss Margo?"

Elizabeth shrugs.

"Come on!" I say.

She sighs and flutters her eyelids. "Maybe I didn't
ask her. Maybe I didn't want to share a room with her
daughter, who hides moldy old peanut butter sandwiches under her bed. Maybe I don't want to do yard

work every day like I'm some kind of indentured servant."

"If you didn't ask her, how come you know all that?" I ask as I pull my shirt over my head. I'm glad to get my shirt back on, glad that Elizabeth didn't say anything about my bra.

"You think I'm an idiot?" She cocks her head and rocks a little. "I'm not going to plan to live with someone without doing a little research first."

This sounds true, but I bet there is more to it than this. This is the way Elizabeth is. She only says part of the truth, the part that leads you to think what she wants you to think. It isn't a lie, exactly, but it doesn't give you a clear sense of the truth, either.

"So, are you going to help or what?"

I shake my head.

"Why not?" She glares at me.

I hand Elizabeth the purple brochure.

She looks it over, outside then in. She inspects every inch as if it is a piece of evidence. "So?"

"So? Don't be stupid. Mom's never liked Pistachio and she hates having him in her car. What do you think she's planning?"

"God, you're lame. Mom's not going to put Pistachio to sleep." She tweaks the brochure with her finger. "This doesn't mean anything. Look! Look what she circled! The part about a trip being hard on old dogs."

"Yeah, that's her excuse."

"Why don't you just talk to her? You never talk to anyone about anything. You just go off half—what does Mom call it—half-cocked. Just like Dad when he gets all bent out of shape and up and quits. Look, she's never going to let you go live with Harrison. So this is our only chance. Will you help or not?"

"Who said I was going to live with Harrison?" I'm mad that she guessed this.

Elizabeth turns her head and looks sideways at me. "Like, duh? What else are you going to do?"

"If you must know, I have a lot of options," I say as I walk back to the kitchen and get the Cheez-It box out of the cupboard. I dig my hand in and pull out the biggest possible handful of orange crackers. "But I will help you, so long as you promise one thing."

"What?" She steals a cracker from me. She breaks it, pops half in her mouth, and tosses the other half back.

"If she tries to take Pistachio, you'll help me."

"What . . . she's going to take him at gunpoint?"

"You have to promise," I say.

"All right, all right, I promise," she says with a swirly twirl and two leaps.

26
ANT

As usual, Elizabeth is making this talk with my mom into a big production. She did my hair in a weird hairdo with bunches of bobby pins that are giving me a headache. She ironed one of my dresses and made me wear shoes. I hate shoes. They bug me to death. And then she spent a good twenty minutes trying to figure out "the location." She said, "You know how the president always goes to the Rose Garden when he makes a nice announcement to give an award or something. But if it's a serious announcement, about bombing, you see him in the Oval Office or the Map Room. This is a Rose Garden talk. The day is perfect for it," she says. It is an incredibly warm day for November, that's for sure. Still, I think she's nuts, but I do what she says. Especially since the nearest thing to the Rose Garden is our backyard. And since Pistachio is allowed back there, this means he can stay with me. This is important.

Now Elizabeth is setting out folding chairs and a card table on the cement. She uses a striped beach towel for a tablecloth and puts a Dixie cup full of yellow wildflowers in the middle. Then she brings out lemonade in a blue plastic pitcher and a plate of rice cakes with jelly. The ice cubes clink against the pitcher when she sets it down. She has even remembered to bring my mom's sunglasses. They are neatly folded by her plate.

"Ant, sit down before Mom comes so she doesn't see you walk."

"What's the matter with the way I walk?"

"Nothing . . . if you like monkeys." Elizabeth hunches her shoulders and swings her arms in front of her as if she's walking on crutches, then jumps her legs forward.

"Come on . . . ," I say, snapping my head back.

Elizabeth ignores me. She is into her performance now. She stands up extra tall, stretches her squat neck to the sky, holds the sides of her skirt, and steps lightly toe-heel, toe-heel, her face smiling like she is being watched by adoring crowds. "*This* is how you *should* walk," she explains.

"Oh yeah, just what I want to be . . . the Sugarplum Fairy," I tell her.

"Shut up, you don't know anything!" She glares at me. Then her face seems to soften. "Trust me, she hates the way you walk, so sit down and don't move. And be nice. BE NICE! I'm not going to get her until you promise." She crosses her arms.

I make a scoffing noise, but I sit down. "I'll be nice," I say, "but I don't walk like any monkey."

"Fine. Okay," Elizabeth says. She gestures with her

hands as if this is the end of it, then she gets up and leaves me and Pistachio alone.

I am petting him when my mom comes out. She sees me sitting in the chair, with the table, the flowers, and the lemonade. The corners of her mouth turn up. It is a small smile and it only lasts two blinks, but in it I see something that surprises me. My mother is glad to see me. Me. I smile back, before I catch myself. Do not do this, I tell myself. The second Elizabeth or Kate shows up, you'll be couch food again.

My mom touches her hair as if to check that it is in place and sits down. I pour us each a glass of lemonade and offer her a rice cake with jelly, just like Elizabeth said to. My mom crosses her legs. "So, what's this all about?" she asks.

Elizabeth has told me not to mention the thing about Pistachio until the end, but this is where I start, though I do take Elizabeth's advice on how to ask. I say the words exactly as Elizabeth scripted them for me.

"I found this flyer on the kitchen desk. I wasn't snooping, it was just there, out in the open. And when I saw it . . . it worried me." I hand the folded-up flyer to my mother.

My mom opens the flyer. When she sees what it says, her face gets tense. She frowns, shakes her head, and sighs. Then she looks out at her yellow pansies and back at Pistachio, curled in my lap. She sighs again. "Pistachio seems to be doing okay. We haven't taken him to the vet recently, or at least *I haven't*." She looks at me.

"I haven't, either," I say.

"I don't think it's time to euthanize him, if that's what you're worried about." She looks at me again.

"You mean *murder* him," I say, but as soon as the words pop out of my mouth, I am sorry I've said them.

My mother makes an annoyed sound in her throat. Here we go again, I think. But then she seems to regain her cool. "I am concerned about how we're going to get him to Connecticut, though. I'm afraid we may need to fly him there."

"In an airplane?" I say. I can't believe my mother is suggesting spending money on Pistachio.

"It's tax deductible," she offers.

That figures, I think, but this time I manage to hold my tongue.

"And then I don't know if Pistachio will have to be quarantined. It's one of the one hundred things I have to find out about. I got that flyer because it talks about how old dogs can be traumatized by a move. I wanted to show your dad because I'm worried if something happens to him, you'll never forgive us."

I look at her. I'm surprised she has thought about this. Amazed, actually.

She shakes her head. "You and that teacher of yours act like I never think about you . . . like I don't know how attached you are to that dog. I'd have to be blind, deaf, and dumb not to see that. The way I figure it, I better make sure nothing happens to Pistachio or it'll be a Lizzie Borden situation."

"Lizzie Borden?"

"Decapitated her parents with an ax."

"God, Mom!"

"It's a joke, Antonia." She smiles. She seems pleased with herself. "What"—she looks over the top of her sunglasses—"you never heard of Lizzie Borden?"

I shake my head.

"You got an A in history. I thought you might have heard of Lizzie Borden. You did get an A in history, didn't you?"

I nod.

She seems reassured. "You're a puzzling child, you know that? And sometimes, you make me so angry, I could tear my hair out." She pulls at her neat blond hair.

I look at her. Her chin is resting on her fingertips. Her brown eyes are watching me. She seems to take me in from head to toe, as if I am someone she hasn't seen before. "You look nice in that dress, Antonia."

"Thank you," I say. It feels good to hear her say this. I try to block how good it feels, but I can't. Something inside me has softened and I can't make it hard again.

"As a matter of fact, you look a little like I did when I was eleven." She smiles.

"I do?" I look down at myself.

"Your hair and that nose . . ." She bites her lip. "Gosh, I hated my nose when I was your age and I hated my mouse brown hair. You know, honey, you shouldn't worry about your nose. We can do something about that when you get older."

I reach for my nose. "I like my hair *and* my nose," I say, protecting it with my hand.

She sighs. "Well, fine then," she says, her eyebrows raised high, her jaw hard.

"Mom?"

"Yes?"

"When I was a baby, did you love me . . . or did you hate my nose then, too?" I shouldn't have said this about the nose. It is mean and angry.

Her neck stiffens. "That's not fair," she says. "I don't hate your nose now. I'm just . . ." She sighs and shakes her head. "Oh, never mind. Forget I said anything."

"No. I want to know. Did you love me when I was a baby?"

"Of course I did. Of course," she says, looking into my eyes.

I can't look at her. I look down. I don't say anything for a long time. I am trying to remember what it was like when I was little. What she was like.

"I did, Antonia. I did."

"You used to sing to me, I remember that," I say.

"Uh-huh. I remember that, too. You always liked when I sang. I'd sing a song and you'd giggle and smile and clap your little hands together as if I was the best singer you ever heard."

"And when you said good night to me, you'd say 'Don't let the bedbugs bite.' "

She nods. She is watching me now. We sit quietly, both of us. It's nice, remembering this. But then I have to speak again. I have to. "Mom?"

"Uh-huh."

"What happened?"

Her jaw stiffens. Her lips clamp back into their hard line. *"Nothing happened."*

This is not true and we both know it. I wait. She looks at me. I run my hand over and over Pistachio's head. I wait some more. I want to know. I have to know.

"You're a tough one, Antonia. You fight me on everything. Everything I do—*everything* is wrong. And the lies . . . I can't trust anything you say."

I bite my tongue when she says this so I won't argue, so I will let it pass. This is not the real thing. I want to know the real thing. "Mom?"

"Yes?"

"How come you love Elizabeth and Kate more than me?"

She bristles. "I don't." Her eyes are hard and mad. "I love all you girls the same."

"No." I choke on the word as it comes out.

She looks away—out to her yellow pansies. The flower bed is close, but her eyes seem to see through to a distant spot. She is quiet for a long time. Then I see her fingers dab the corners of her eyes. She is crying. I try to remember if I have ever seen her cry. The tears are spilling out faster than she can dab them. She searches in her pocket for a Kleenex and blows her nose in that delicate way she has and cleans the tears off her face.

She starts again, "They do what I tell them. You never do. With you, I'm always *the villain.*" She has to stop again because she's crying so much.

I look down at Pistachio, his little triangle ears and sweet brown eyes. *He* loves me.

"Even when you were little . . . I'd send you to preschool in the morning, brand-new clothes, all neat and clean, cute as a button just like I wish my mom had done for me, and you'd come home filthy from head to toe, belt torn off your dress, shoes on the wrong feet, nose bloody. Your teacher would say you got in a fight. That was always the first thing you did when someone did something you didn't like. You'd punch 'em. And not some nice polite little hit, either. You'd really go after them."

Well, they probably deserved it, I think. But I do not say this. She is going somewhere with this. I let her finish.

"Do you know how embarrassing it is to have a little girl who is always getting in trouble? You were kicked out of two preschools, you know that? I was mortified. And then you started the lying business. You'd tell some elaborate story about how you were the queen of Egypt's daughter. The queen of Egypt? Where do you get these things?" She shakes her head. "No one can ever believe you are Elizabeth's sister. She is such a good child. And Kate is, too. But you . . ." She dabs at her nose with her Kleenex. "Of course I prefer them. Who wouldn't? Who wouldn't?"

Something inside me goes cold and hard. I stop hearing, stop seeing. I crawl inside myself to where it is safe. I think about my real mother and how I am her favorite. I don't care that she isn't real. I think about Just Carol and how she picked me and not Joyce Ann Jensen. I think about Harrison and how I am his best friend. I imagine a time in the future when my mother tells me how wrong she was this day, today.

"I am smarter than Elizabeth and Kate," I say. "I am!"

"But then *that teacher* comes along," my mother continues. "She really likes you. She thinks you are bright and funny and in a lot of pain. She thinks there's something wrong at home. That I haven't given you any ground to stand on. That I've set up, what did she call it, 'a no-win situation' for you. That it's too hard for you to be good when Elizabeth and Kate have already claimed that title. That you've dug yourself in so deep, you can't get out. That you aren't tough at all. In fact, you're pretty darn fragile. She doesn't know what happened before, but now all your lying is pretty much confined to lies to protect a dog you love more than life itself and fantasies about your real parents."

"Fantasies?" I shake my head no. My real parents may not be real, but they sure as heck aren't fantasies. Fantasies are what crazy people have.

"I tell Just Carol she's wrong. What she says sounds like a bunch of psychobabble, a big load of horse manure. Then I find out you're the District 2 Champion in math and you got almost all A's on your last report card, only you brought home Harrison's so I wouldn't know. And I begin to see your lies usually are about Pistachio. That when we set up a way for you to feel like you're taking good care of him, things do get better. And I think that maybe, maybe Miss Carol Samberson, fresh out of college, is not so far wrong."

She is still crying. Every minute or so she mops the new tears with her Kleenex. Her mascara is dripping down her face in big black rivers. She closes her eyes and the tears stream out of the messy black lashes.

I wonder why she is crying so hard. I know she hates being wrong . . . but would that make her cry this much?

"Antonia . . . ," she says, her eyes still closed. She bites her lip. Her voice breaks. "What I'm trying to say is I'm sorry."

For a second I have to think about how to breathe. I open my mouth. Now I'm breathing, but my chest is still packed solid, and all I can think about is what it would feel like to hug my mother. I know that Elizabeth and Kate do. But not me. I must have hugged her when I was little. I know I hugged my father. But I don't remember ever putting my arms around my mother. I wonder if she is thinking about hugging me now.

"Mom," I say. My voice sounds funny. It echoes in my ears as if I have a head cold. It sounds far away from me. "I'm sorry, too," I say. No, I'm not, I think. I'm not. This is all a big lie. But it is not a lie. It is the truth. This is my real mother. I wish she were different. She wishes I were different. But that doesn't mean she's not mine.

"Mom," I ask, "will you call me Ant?"

"Oh, Antonia," my mother sighs. Her face looks pained. She is quiet for a few moments and then she says, "Antonia is such a lovely name. When I named you, you were the sweetest, most perfect little baby. I never dreamed you'd want to shorten Antonia to Ant.

Tony, I could see. Tony I could live with. Tony is kind of cute. How about Tony?"

"My name is Ant," I say. I look in her eyes, past where I usually look to a spot inside.

My mother is silent. She stares off across the street. Then she looks back at me. Her mouth tries a little smile, she covers her hand with my hand. "All right . . . Ant," she says.

We sit this way for a minute. I think about pulling my hand away, but I don't. I don't.

"Maybe this move will be good for us," she says. "It will give us a fresh start."

My stomach dips down. I feel the blood drain from my face. I jerk my hand away. I'd forgotten all about the move and what it was I was supposed to be talking to her about.

"No," I say. This comes out louder than I mean it to. My mother's eyes grow suddenly wary.

"We move too much. It isn't good for . . ." I try to think who to name here. I settle on: "Pistachio."

Her eyes dart away again, as if it is too painful to look at me.

"How come we have to move all the time? How come Dad doesn't stay long at any job?"

My mother shakes her head. Her lips are pressed together. She dabs at her eyes as if she's trying not to cry. But she is crying.

"I need to stay here in Sarah's Road with Harrison and Just Carol . . ." I try to say the last, but I can't. I start again. "I need to stay here with Harrison and Just Carol and Daddy and Elizabeth and Kate . . ." I think I will end here, but my voice keeps going. I try to stop the words, but they bubble up from deep inside. "I need to stay here with you," I say. My voice cracks. I bite my tongue and open my eyes wide so I won't cry. But I can't keep the tears back. They chase each other down my cheeks.

She squeezes my hand. We are quiet for a long time, listening to distant noises. The traffic sounds from Sarah's Road, the sassy voice of a radio disc jockey, the mechanical drill of a power saw, and our own sniffling.

I look at her. Her brown eyes are glossy with tears. Every time she looks at me, the tears spill over again.

She is trying. She is. And so am I.

27
THE FACTS

I've tried to imagine the conversation that happened later that day—the one between my mom and my dad. I think about it as I clean the kennels in the vet's office or sit listening to Cave Man in math class or say goodbye to Harrison when he's going to the zoo, where he's allowed and I'm not. Usually I imagine the discussion happening late at night when Kate and Elizabeth and me are all asleep, and the only sounds in the house are the hum of the refrigerator and the tick of the heater turning on. I picture my mom and my dad sitting in the living room watching TV. I see my mom click the power off and the screen go suddenly blue and blank. I imagine her turning to my dad and saying: "I don't want to move to Connecticut, Don."

And then my father smiles his salesman smile and says, "Oh, honey. You'll love it there. You just wait."

But this is made up, of course. The only facts I have to work with are these. The week after my mom and I had our talk, my father turned down the job in Connecticut and accepted a position close to home. Then, my mother unpacked all the boxes in the garage and she planted two trees in our backyard. That's it. That's all I know, but I spend an awful lot of time wondering about the rest.

What I can't figure out is why my mother told my father she didn't want to go. Is it because my mom hates icy winters and sticky summers? Is it because of Elizabeth and her performance schedule at Miss Marion Margo's? Or is it because of me? I think about this almost every day. I shouldn't, though. I know I shouldn't. Because I really don't want to know the answer to this question unless the answer is me.